MANGA MATH MYSTERIES #4

THE KUNG FU PUZZLE

A Mystery with Time and Temperature

by Melinda Thielbar

illustrated by Der-shing Helmer

GRAPHIC UNIVERSE™ · MINNEAPOLIS

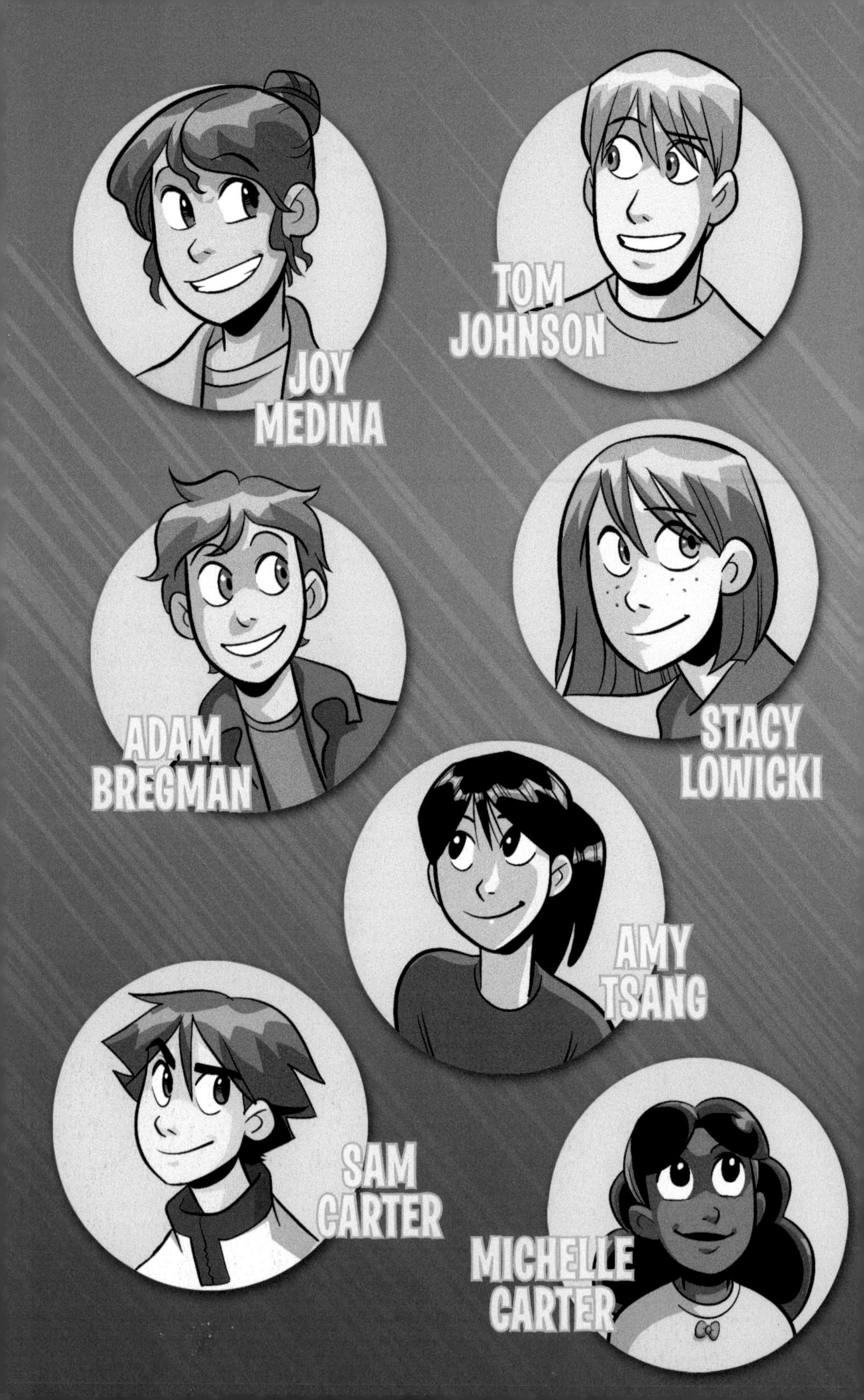
JOY
MEDINA
TOM
JOHNSON
ADAM
BREGMAN
STACY
LOWICKI
AMY
TSANG
SAM
CARTER
MICHELLE
CARTER

SIFU FAIZA

SIGUNG

BRIAN NARATA

SAM'S DAD

How do we measure **time**? We measure time in seconds, minutes, and hours. We read time on two kinds of clocks. An **analog** clock has a minute hand and an hour hand and sometimes a second hand. A **digital** clock shows us the numbers for the hour and minutes.

How do we measure **temperature**? We measure temperature on a **thermometer**. There are two ways to measure temperature. In the United States, we measure temperature in degrees **Fahrenheit**. In other parts of the world, temperature is measured in degrees **Celsius**.

Story by Melinda Thielbar
Pencils and inks by Der-shing Helmer
Coloring by Hi-Fi Design
Lettering by Marshall Dillon

Graphic Universe™
A division of Lerner Publishing Group, Inc.
241 First Avenue North
Minneapolis, MN 55401 USA

For reading levels and more information, look up this title at www.lernerbooks.com.

Library of Congress Cataloging-in-Publication Data

Thielbar, Melinda.
   The kung fu puzzle : a mystery with time and temperature / by Melinda Thielbar ; illustrated by Der-shing Helmer.
       p.   cm. — (Manga math mysteries)
   Summary: Sam and his friends at the kung fu school use mathematics to solve puzzles about boiling water and melting glass, and figure out the secret to opening a clock that is really a lock while helping Sifu Faiza.
       ISBN: 978-0-7613-3856-7 (lib. bdg. : alk. paper)
       ISBN: 978-0-7613-5736-0 (eb pdf)
       1. Graphic novels. [1. Graphic novels. 2. Mystery and detective stories. 3. Mathematics—Fiction. 4. Kung fu—Fiction. 5. Schools—Fiction.] I. Helmer, Der-shing, ill. II. Title.
   PZ7.7.T48Ku 2010
   741.5—dc22   2008055564

Manufactured in the United States of America
4 - 43777 - 10013 - 6/29/2021

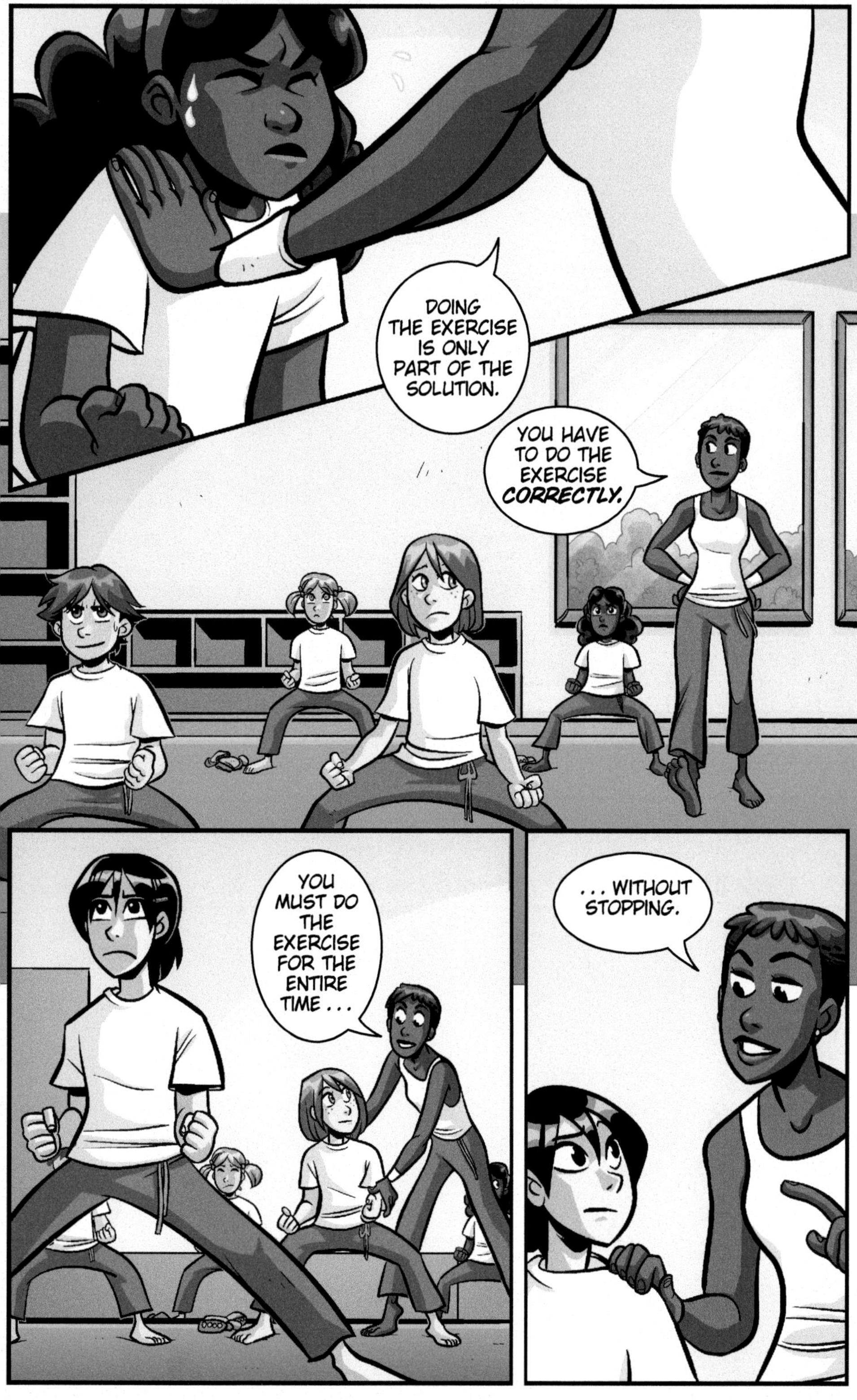
DOING THE EXERCISE IS ONLY PART OF THE SOLUTION.
YOU HAVE TO DO THE EXERCISE *CORRECTLY.*
YOU MUST DO THE EXERCISE FOR THE ENTIRE TIME . . .
. . . WITHOUT STOPPING.

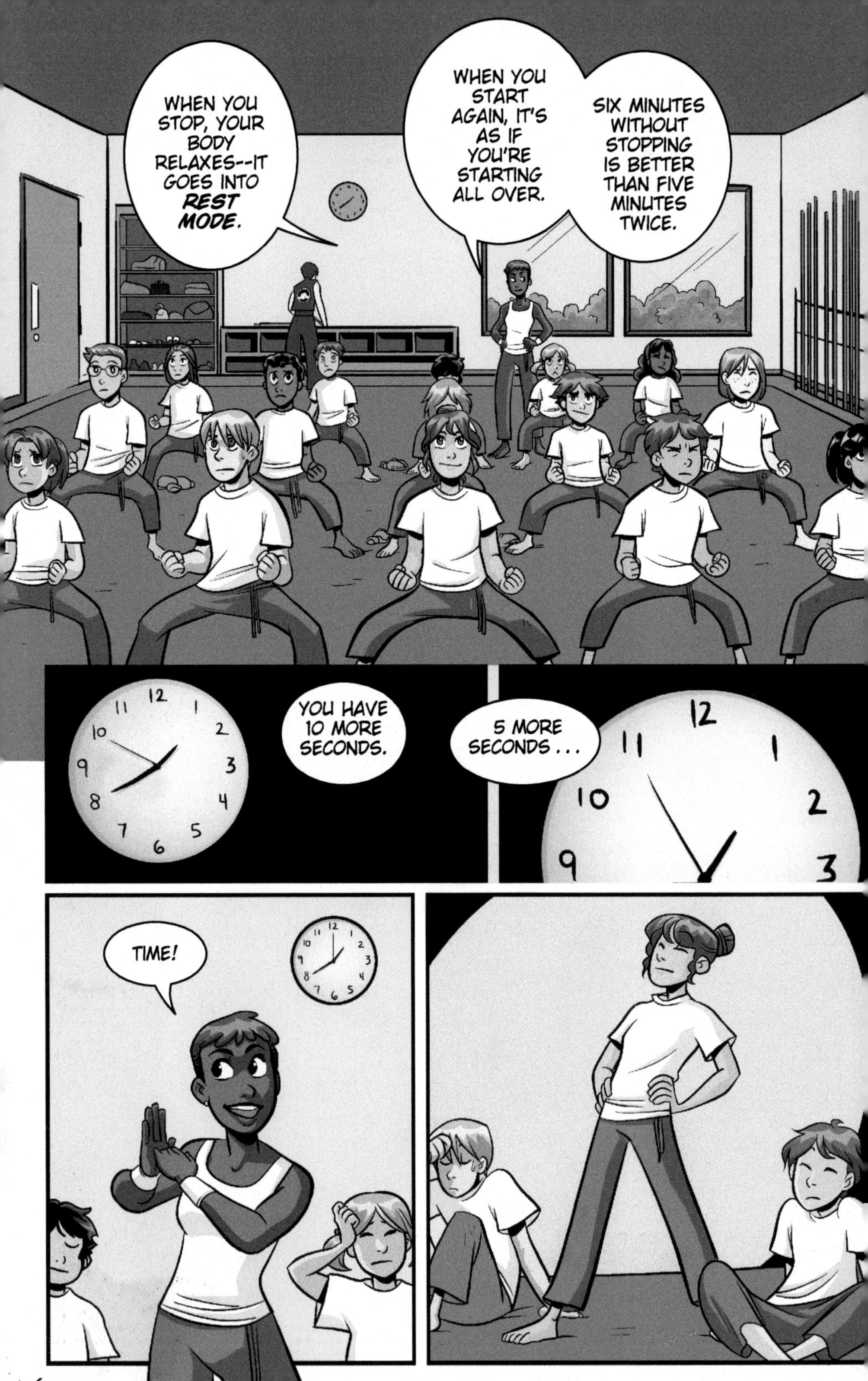
WHEN YOU STOP, YOUR BODY RELAXES--IT GOES INTO ***REST MODE***.
WHEN YOU START AGAIN, IT'S AS IF YOU'RE STARTING ALL OVER.
SIX MINUTES WITHOUT STOPPING IS BETTER THAN FIVE MINUTES TWICE.
YOU HAVE 10 MORE SECONDS.
5 MORE SECONDS . . .
TIME!

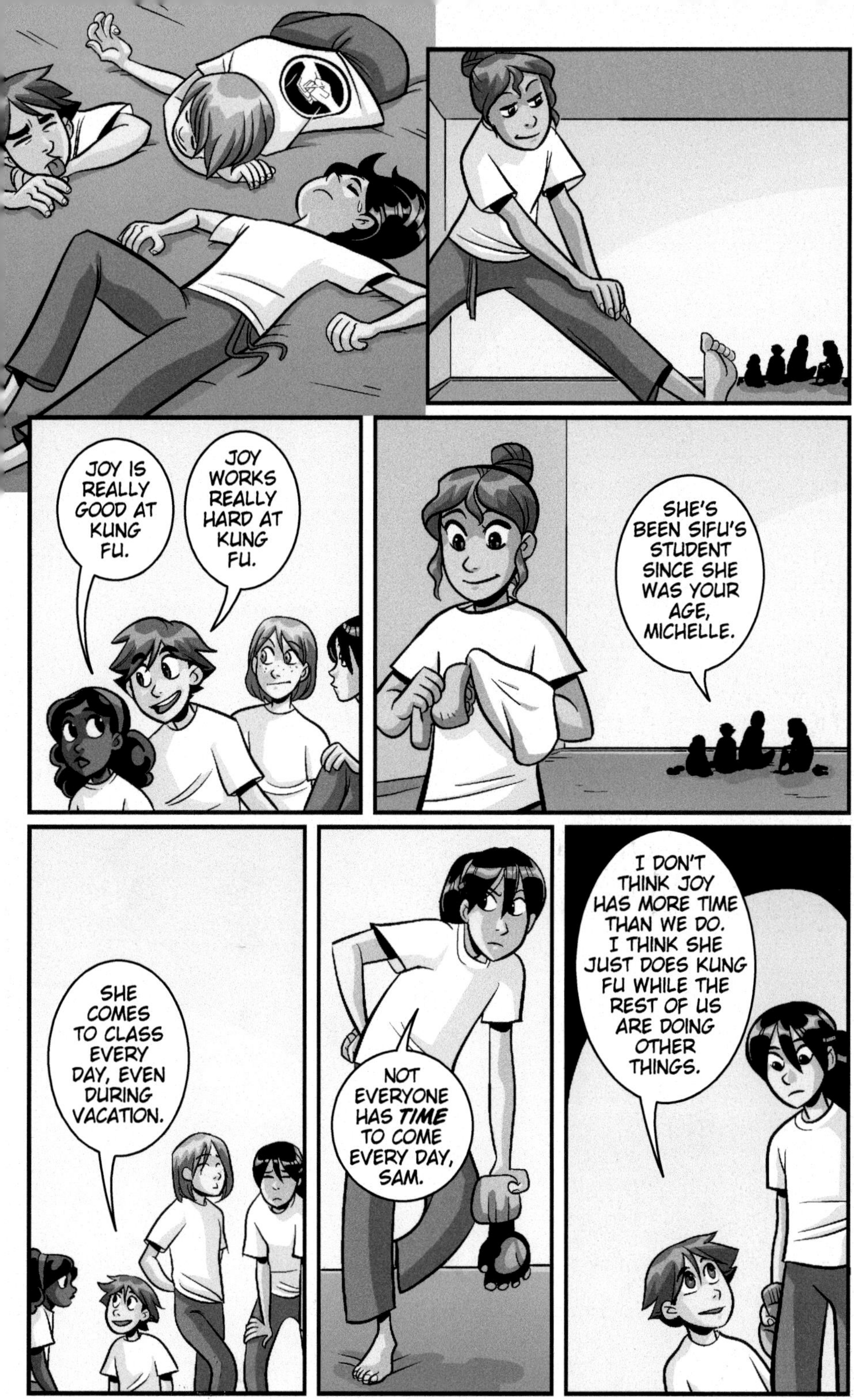
JOY IS REALLY GOOD AT KUNG FU.
JOY WORKS REALLY HARD AT KUNG FU.
SHE'S BEEN SIFU'S STUDENT SINCE SHE WAS YOUR AGE, MICHELLE.
SHE COMES TO CLASS EVERY DAY, EVEN DURING VACATION.
NOT EVERYONE HAS *TIME* TO COME EVERY DAY, SAM.
I DON'T THINK JOY HAS MORE TIME THAN WE DO. I THINK SHE JUST DOES KUNG FU WHILE THE REST OF US ARE DOING OTHER THINGS.

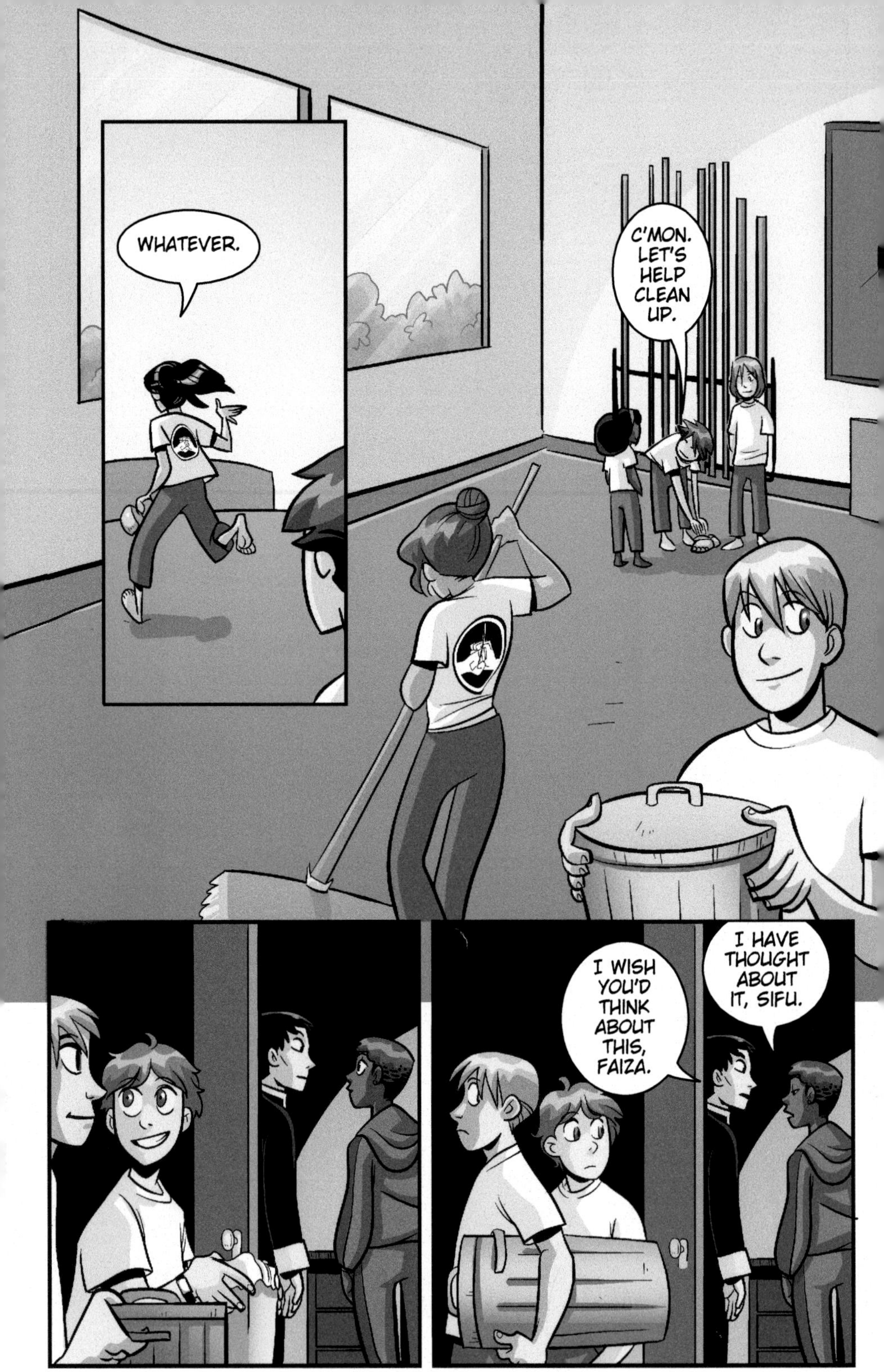
WHATEVER.
C'MON. LET'S HELP CLEAN UP.
I WISH YOU'D THINK ABOUT THIS, FAIZA.
I HAVE THOUGHT ABOUT IT, SIFU.

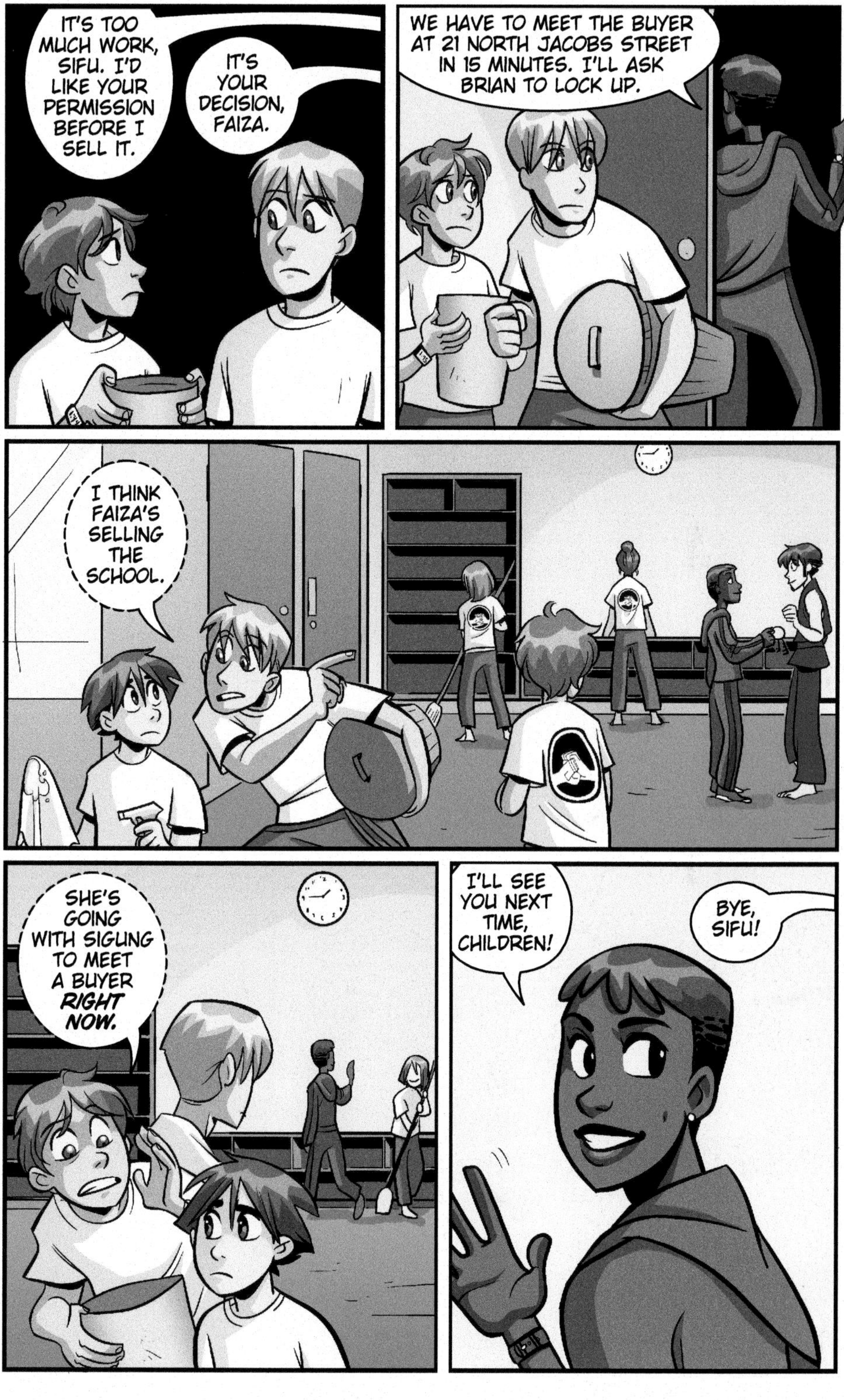
IT'S TOO MUCH WORK, SIFU. I'D LIKE YOUR PERMISSION BEFORE I SELL IT.
IT'S YOUR DECISION, FAIZA.
WE HAVE TO MEET THE BUYER AT 21 NORTH JACOBS STREET IN 15 MINUTES. I'LL ASK BRIAN TO LOCK UP.
I THINK FAIZA'S SELLING THE SCHOOL.
SHE'S GOING WITH SIGUNG TO MEET A BUYER ***RIGHT NOW.***
I'LL SEE YOU NEXT TIME, CHILDREN!
BYE, SIFU!

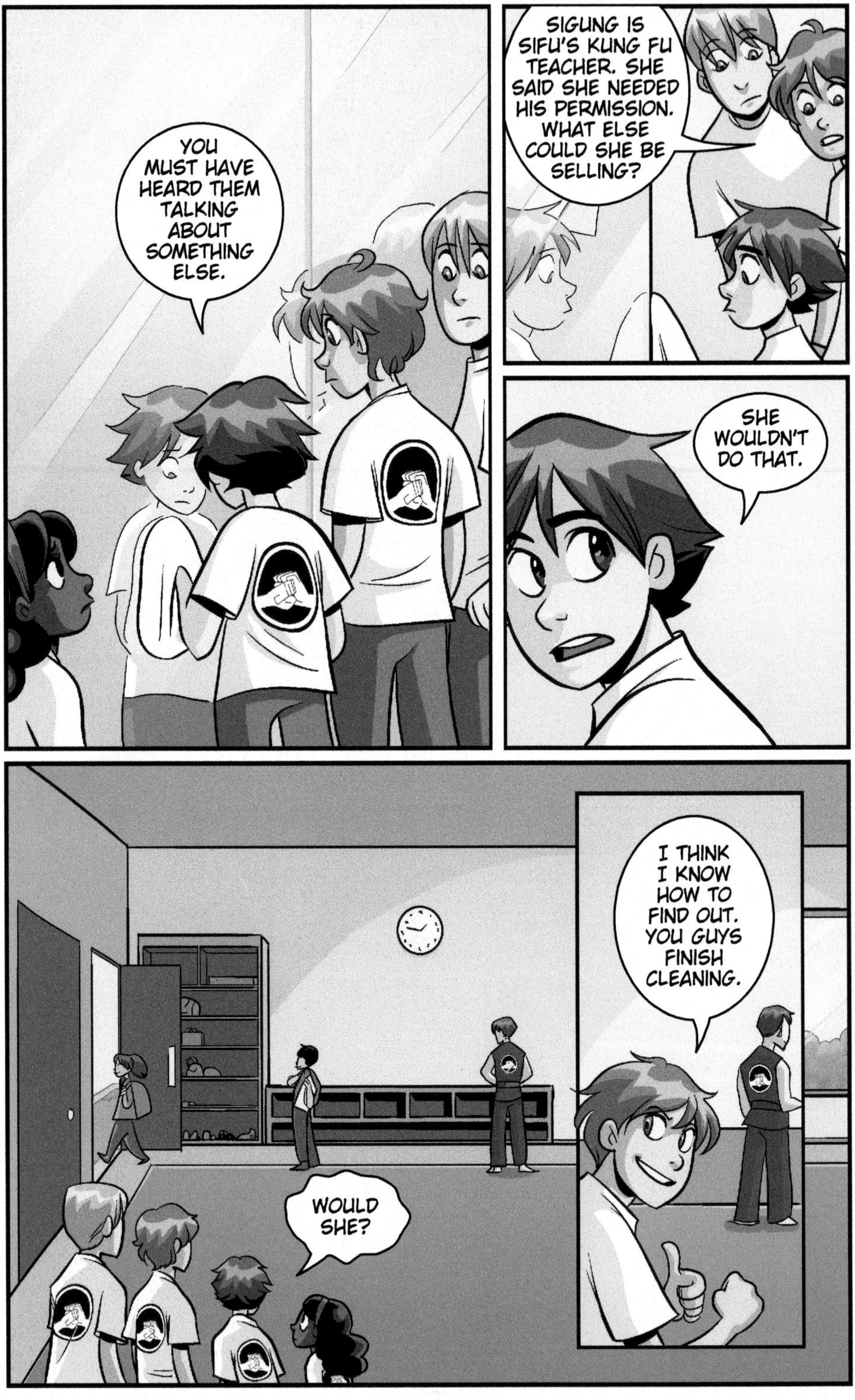
YOU MUST HAVE HEARD THEM TALKING ABOUT SOMETHING ELSE.
SIGUNG IS SIFU'S KUNG FU TEACHER. SHE SAID SHE NEEDED HIS PERMISSION. WHAT ELSE COULD SHE BE SELLING?
SHE WOULDN'T DO THAT.
WOULD SHE?
I THINK I KNOW HOW TO FIND OUT. YOU GUYS FINISH CLEANING.

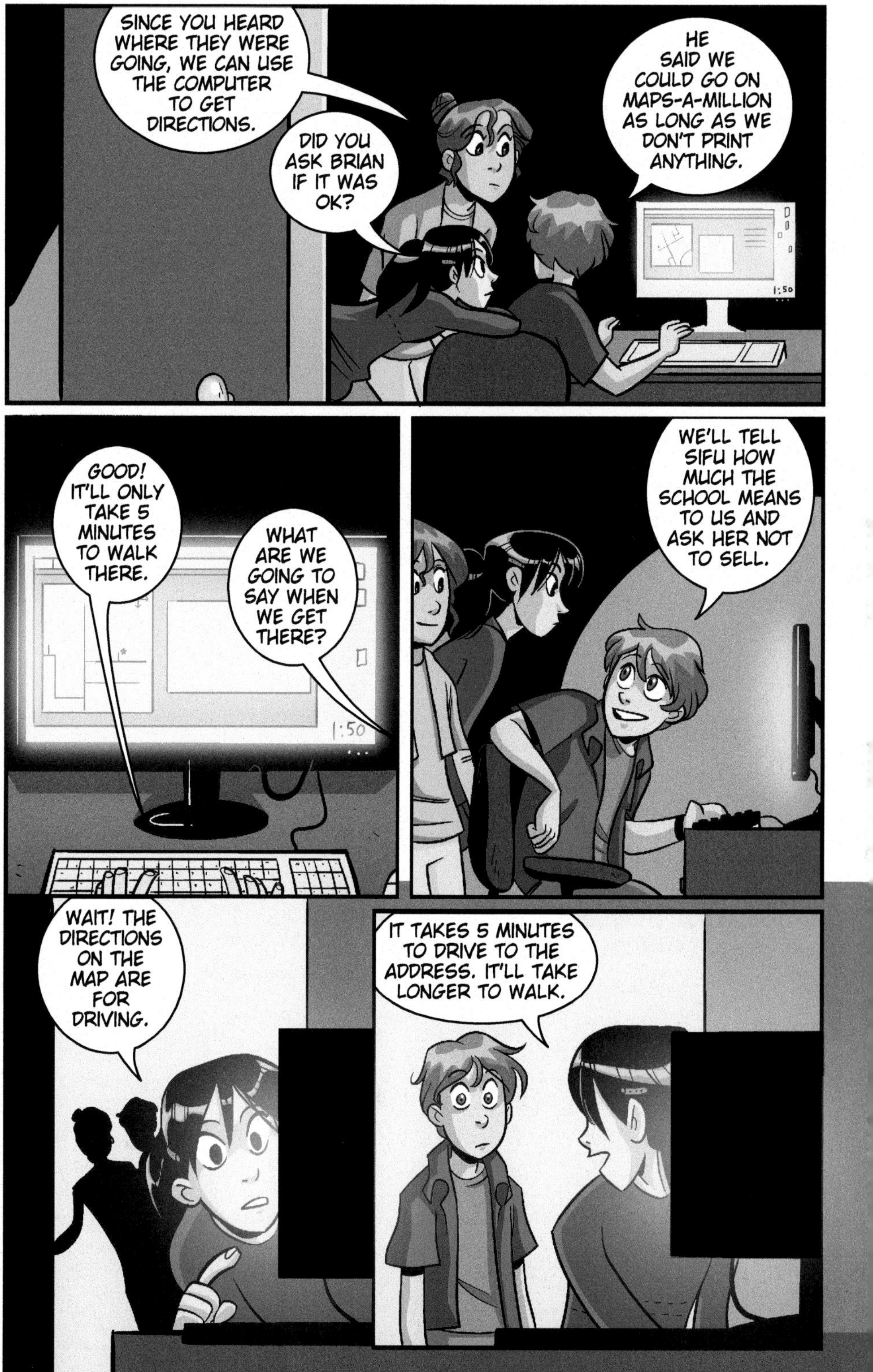
SINCE YOU HEARD WHERE THEY WERE GOING, WE CAN USE THE COMPUTER TO GET DIRECTIONS.
DID YOU ASK BRIAN IF IT WAS OK?
HE SAID WE COULD GO ON MAPS-A-MILLION AS LONG AS WE DON'T PRINT ANYTHING.
1:50
GOOD! IT'LL ONLY TAKE 5 MINUTES TO WALK THERE.
WHAT ARE WE GOING TO SAY WHEN WE GET THERE?
1:50
WE'LL TELL SIFU HOW MUCH THE SCHOOL MEANS TO US AND ASK HER NOT TO SELL.
WAIT! THE DIRECTIONS ON THE MAP ARE FOR DRIVING.
IT TAKES 5 MINUTES TO DRIVE TO THE ADDRESS. IT'LL TAKE LONGER TO WALK.

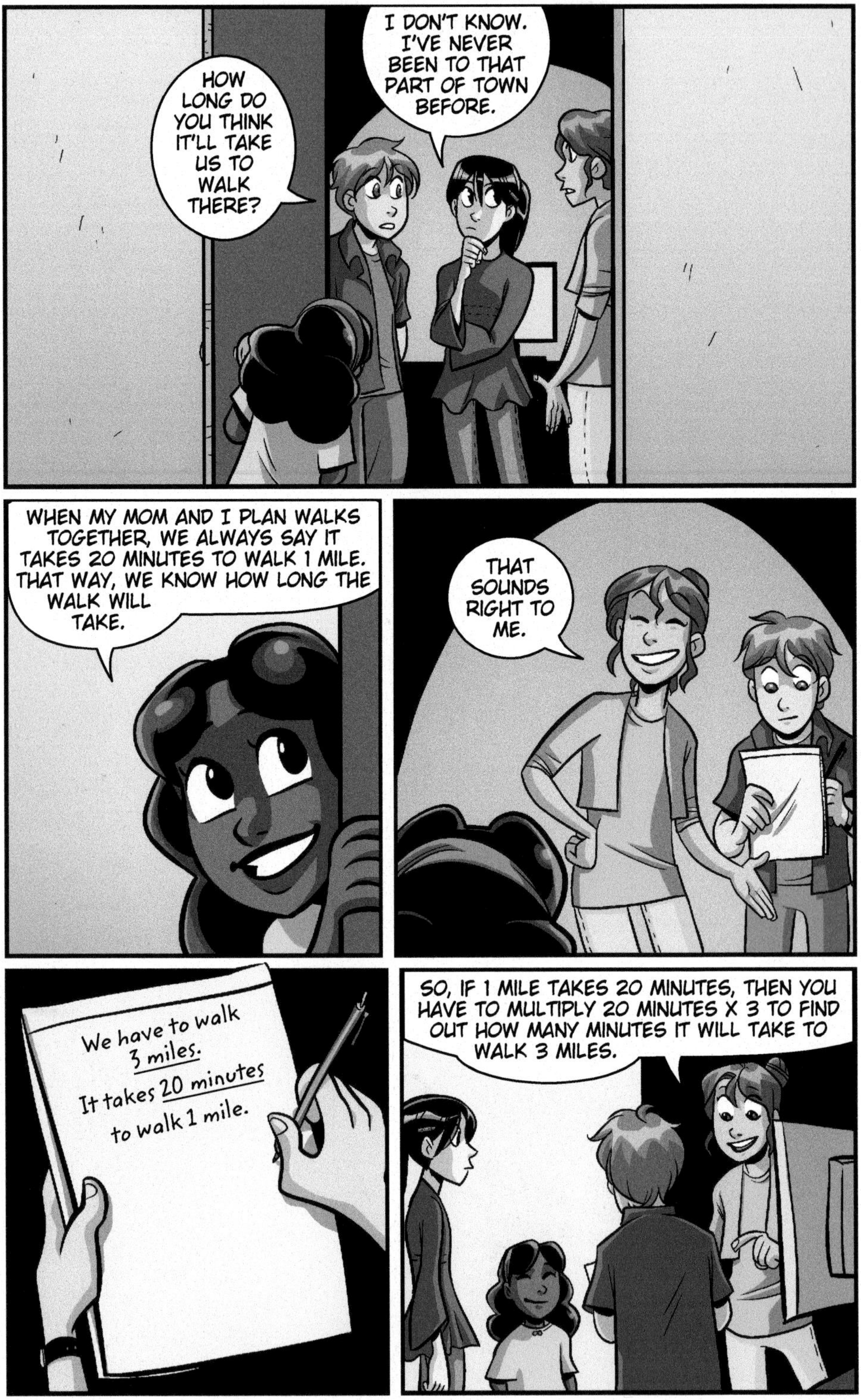
HOW LONG DO YOU THINK IT'LL TAKE US TO WALK THERE?
I DON'T KNOW. I'VE NEVER BEEN TO THAT PART OF TOWN BEFORE.
WHEN MY MOM AND I PLAN WALKS TOGETHER, WE ALWAYS SAY IT TAKES 20 MINUTES TO WALK 1 MILE. THAT WAY, WE KNOW HOW LONG THE WALK WILL TAKE.
THAT SOUNDS RIGHT TO ME.
We have to walk 3 miles. It takes 20 minutes to walk 1 mile.
SO, IF 1 MILE TAKES 20 MINUTES, THEN YOU HAVE TO MULTIPLY 20 MINUTES X 3 TO FIND OUT HOW MANY MINUTES IT WILL TAKE TO WALK 3 MILES.

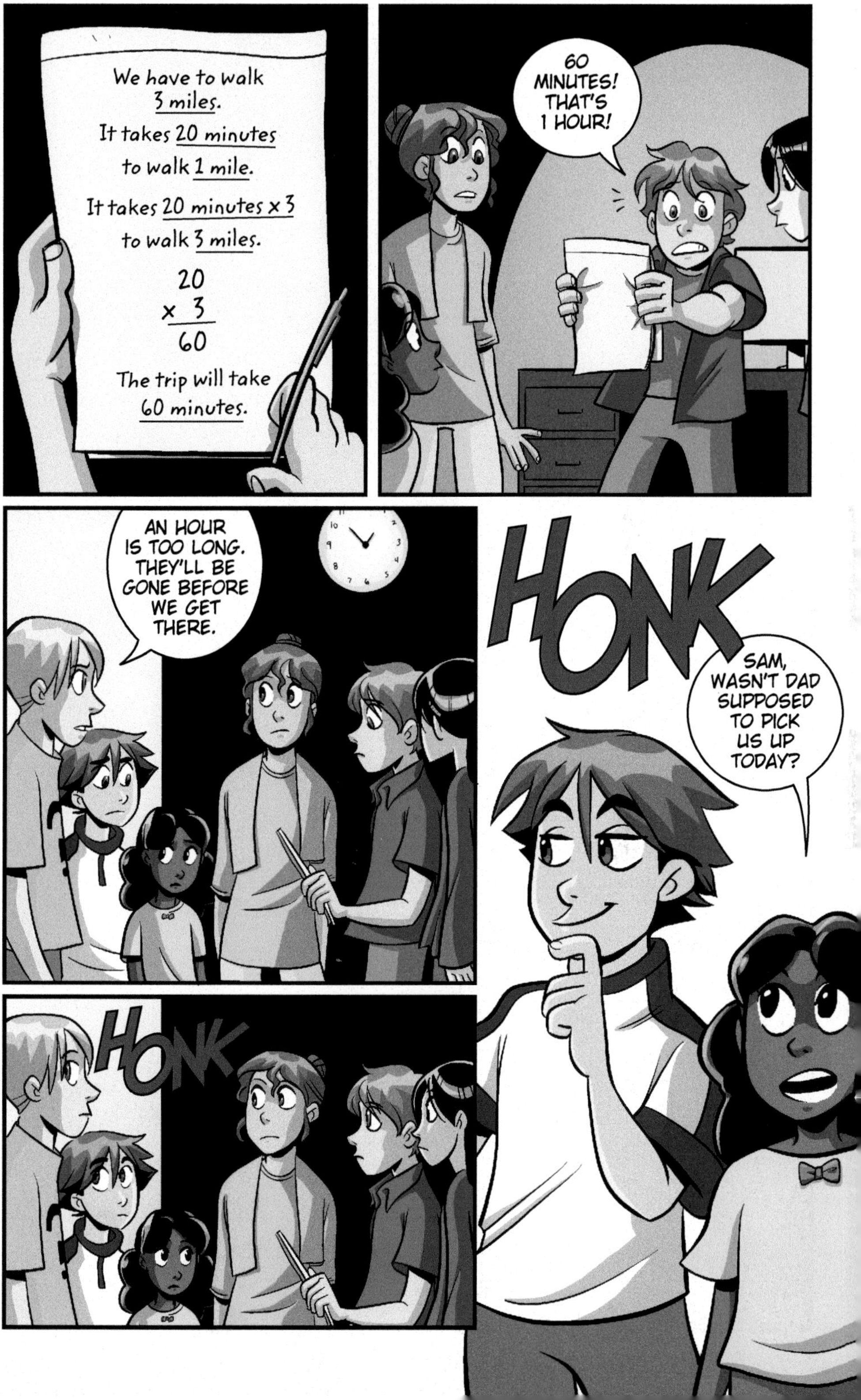
We have to walk 3 miles.
It takes 20 minutes to walk 1 mile.
It takes 20 minutes x 3 to walk 3 miles.
20 x 3 = 60
The trip will take 60 minutes.
60 MINUTES! THAT'S 1 HOUR!
AN HOUR IS TOO LONG. THEY'LL BE GONE BEFORE WE GET THERE.
HONK
HONK
SAM, WASN'T DAD SUPPOSED TO PICK US UP TODAY?

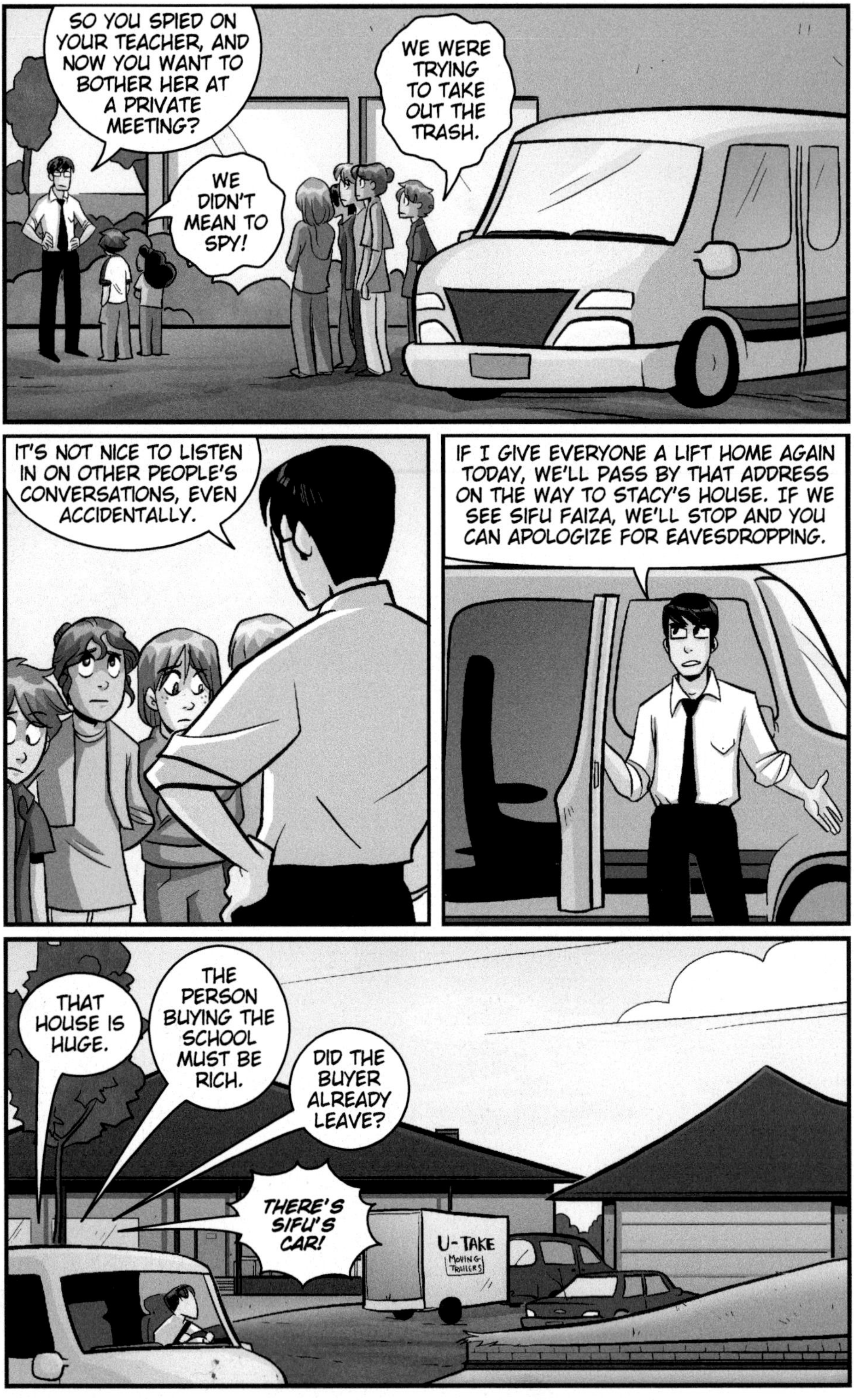
SO YOU SPIED ON YOUR TEACHER, AND NOW YOU WANT TO BOTHER HER AT A PRIVATE MEETING?
WE DIDN'T MEAN TO SPY!
WE WERE TRYING TO TAKE OUT THE TRASH.
IT'S NOT NICE TO LISTEN IN ON OTHER PEOPLE'S CONVERSATIONS, EVEN ACCIDENTALLY.
IF I GIVE EVERYONE A LIFT HOME AGAIN TODAY, WE'LL PASS BY THAT ADDRESS ON THE WAY TO STACY'S HOUSE. IF WE SEE SIFU FAIZA, WE'LL STOP AND YOU CAN APOLOGIZE FOR EAVESDROPPING.
THAT HOUSE IS HUGE.
THE PERSON BUYING THE SCHOOL MUST BE RICH.
DID THE BUYER ALREADY LEAVE?
THERE'S SIFU'S CAR!
U-TAKE
MOVING TRAILERS

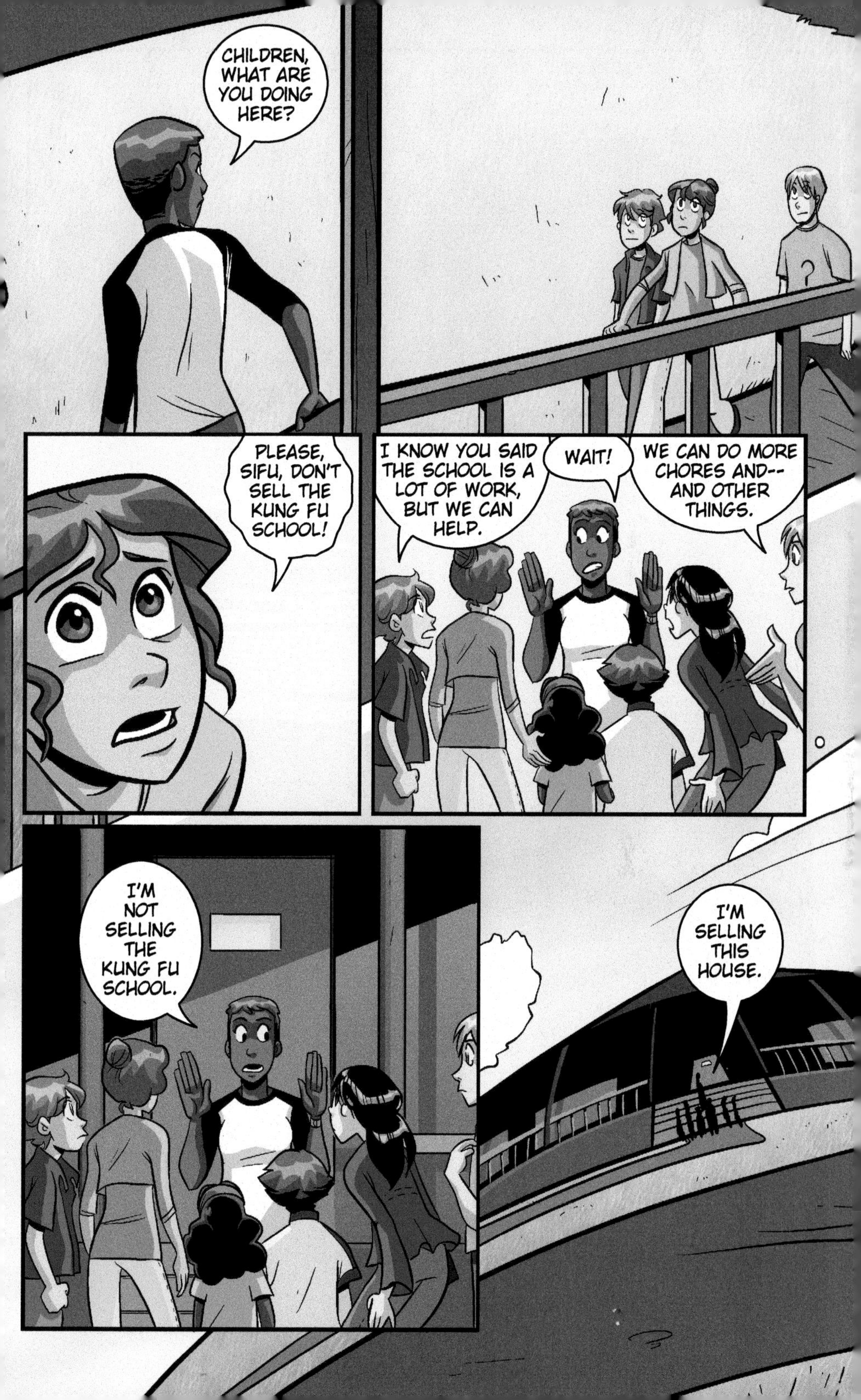
CHILDREN, WHAT ARE YOU DOING HERE?
PLEASE, SIFU, DON'T SELL THE KUNG FU SCHOOL!
I KNOW YOU SAID THE SCHOOL IS A LOT OF WORK, BUT WE CAN HELP.
WAIT!
WE CAN DO MORE CHORES AND-- AND OTHER THINGS.
I'M NOT SELLING THE KUNG FU SCHOOL.
I'M SELLING THIS HOUSE.

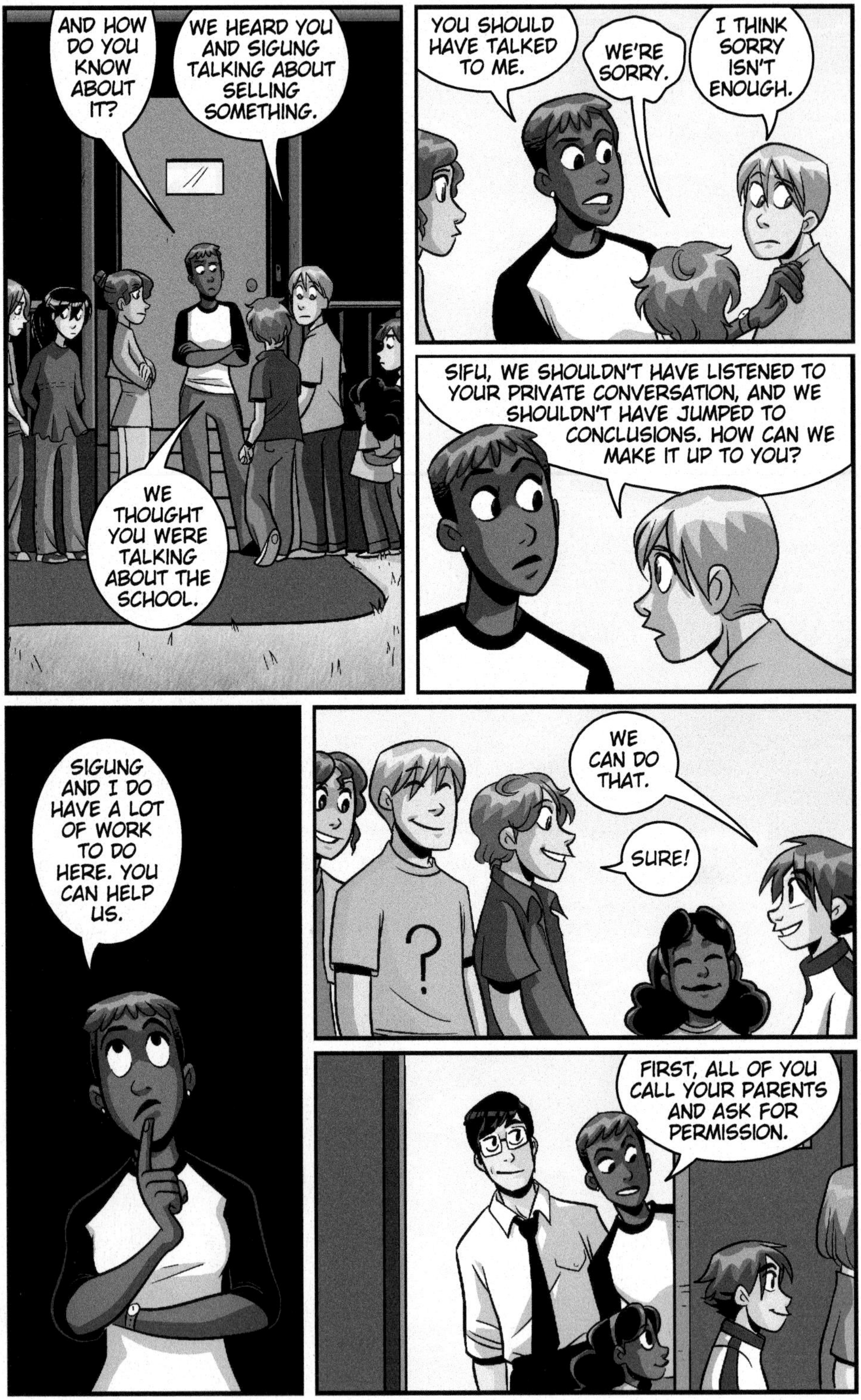
AND HOW DO YOU KNOW ABOUT IT?
WE HEARD YOU AND SIGUNG TALKING ABOUT SELLING SOMETHING.
WE THOUGHT YOU WERE TALKING ABOUT THE SCHOOL.
YOU SHOULD HAVE TALKED TO ME.
WE'RE SORRY.
I THINK SORRY ISN'T ENOUGH.
SIFU, WE SHOULDN'T HAVE LISTENED TO YOUR PRIVATE CONVERSATION, AND WE SHOULDN'T HAVE JUMPED TO CONCLUSIONS. HOW CAN WE MAKE IT UP TO YOU?
SIGUNG AND I DO HAVE A LOT OF WORK TO DO HERE. YOU CAN HELP US.
WE CAN DO THAT.
SURE!
?
FIRST, ALL OF YOU CALL YOUR PARENTS AND ASK FOR PERMISSION.

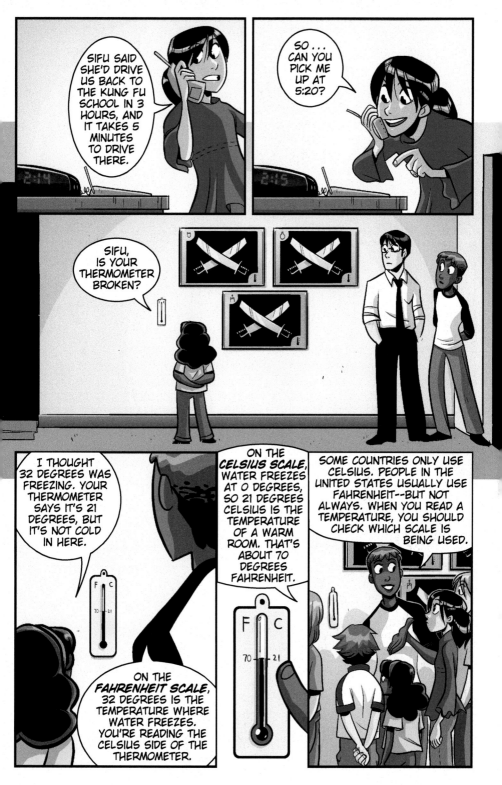

SIFU SAID SHE'D DRIVE US BACK TO THE KUNG FU SCHOOL IN 3 HOURS, AND IT TAKES 5 MINUTES TO DRIVE THERE.

SO... CAN YOU PICK ME UP AT 5:20?

SIFU, IS YOUR THERMOMETER BROKEN?

I THOUGHT 32 DEGREES WAS FREEZING. YOUR THERMOMETER SAYS IT'S 21 DEGREES, BUT IT'S NOT COLD IN HERE.

ON THE *FAHRENHEIT SCALE*, 32 DEGREES IS THE TEMPERATURE WHERE WATER FREEZES. YOU'RE READING THE CELSIUS SIDE OF THE THERMOMETER.

ON THE *CELSIUS SCALE*, WATER FREEZES AT 0 DEGREES, SO 21 DEGREES CELSIUS IS THE TEMPERATURE OF A WARM ROOM. THAT'S ABOUT 70 DEGREES FAHRENHEIT.

SOME COUNTRIES ONLY USE CELSIUS. PEOPLE IN THE UNITED STATES USUALLY USE FAHRENHEIT--BUT NOT ALWAYS. WHEN YOU READ A TEMPERATURE, YOU SHOULD CHECK WHICH SCALE IS BEING USED.

17

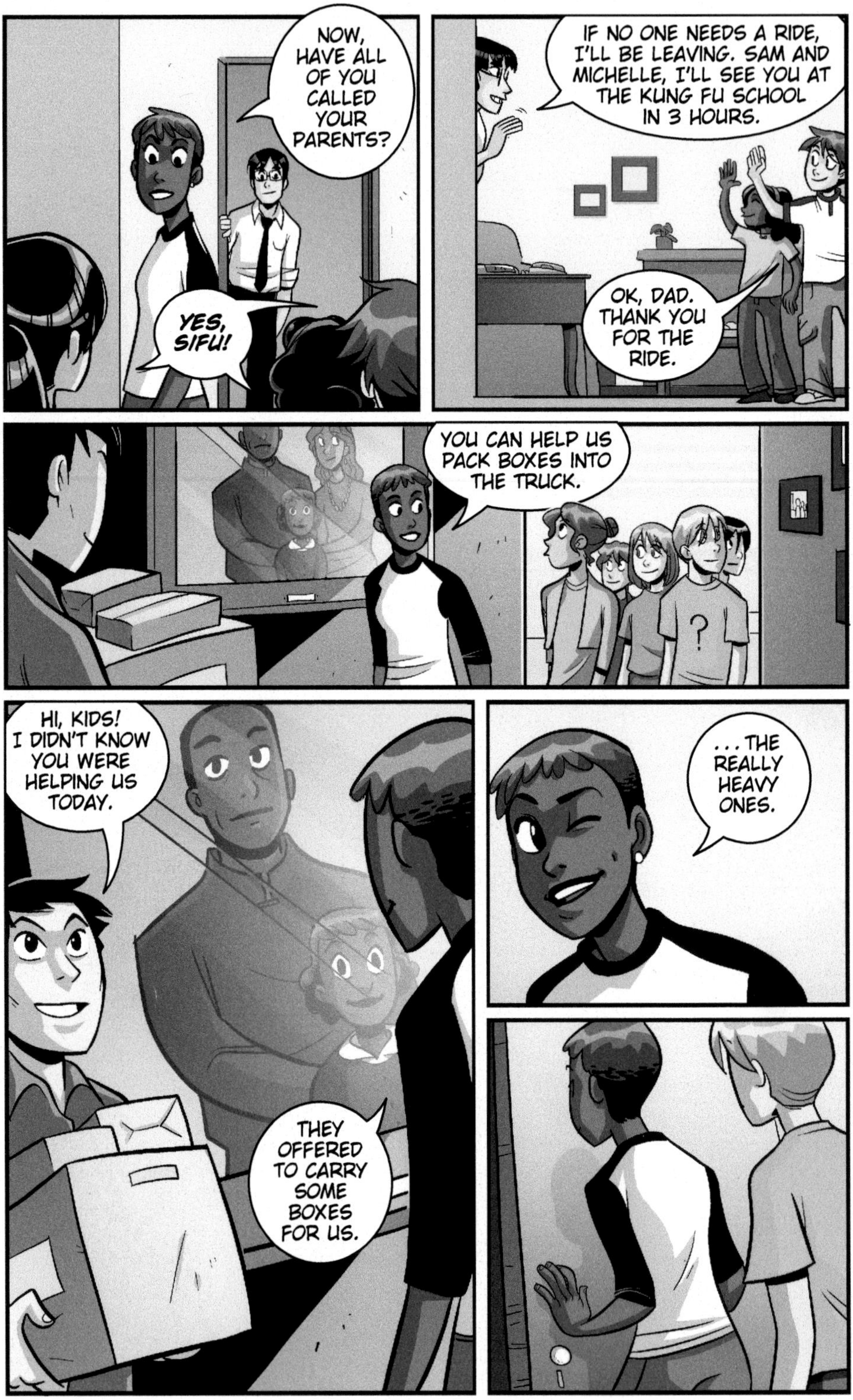
NOW, HAVE ALL OF YOU CALLED YOUR PARENTS?
YES, SIFU!
IF NO ONE NEEDS A RIDE, I'LL BE LEAVING. SAM AND MICHELLE, I'LL SEE YOU AT THE KUNG FU SCHOOL IN 3 HOURS.
OK, DAD. THANK YOU FOR THE RIDE.
YOU CAN HELP US PACK BOXES INTO THE TRUCK.
HI, KIDS! I DIDN'T KNOW YOU WERE HELPING US TODAY.
THEY OFFERED TO CARRY SOME BOXES FOR US.
. . . THE REALLY HEAVY ONES.

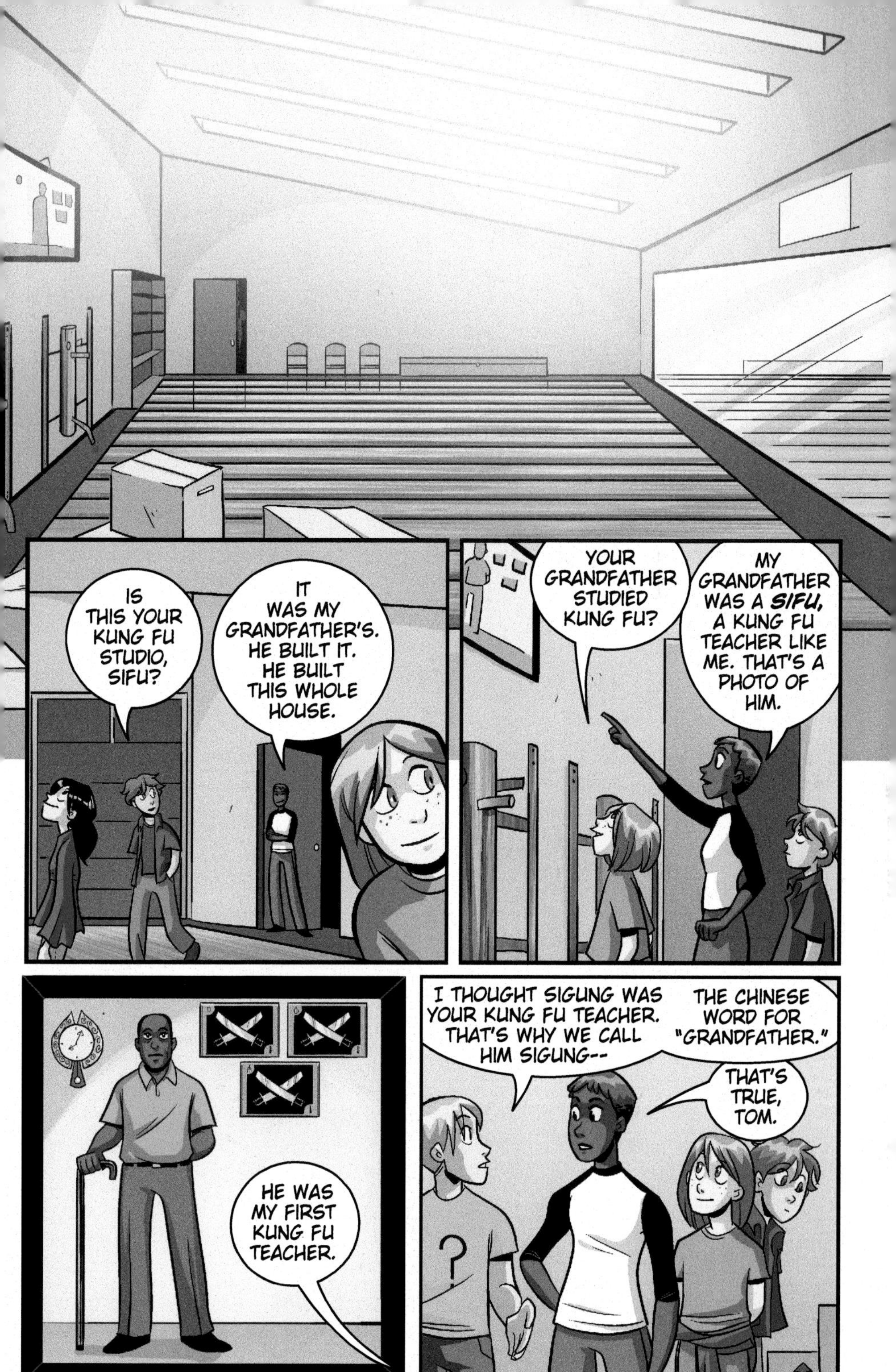
IS THIS YOUR KUNG FU STUDIO, SIFU?
IT WAS MY GRANDFATHER'S. HE BUILT IT. HE BUILT THIS WHOLE HOUSE.
YOUR GRANDFATHER STUDIED KUNG FU?
MY GRANDFATHER WAS A *SIFU,* A KUNG FU TEACHER LIKE ME. THAT'S A PHOTO OF HIM.
HE WAS MY FIRST KUNG FU TEACHER.
I THOUGHT SIGUNG WAS YOUR KUNG FU TEACHER. THAT'S WHY WE CALL HIM SIGUNG--
THE CHINESE WORD FOR "GRANDFATHER."
THAT'S TRUE, TOM.

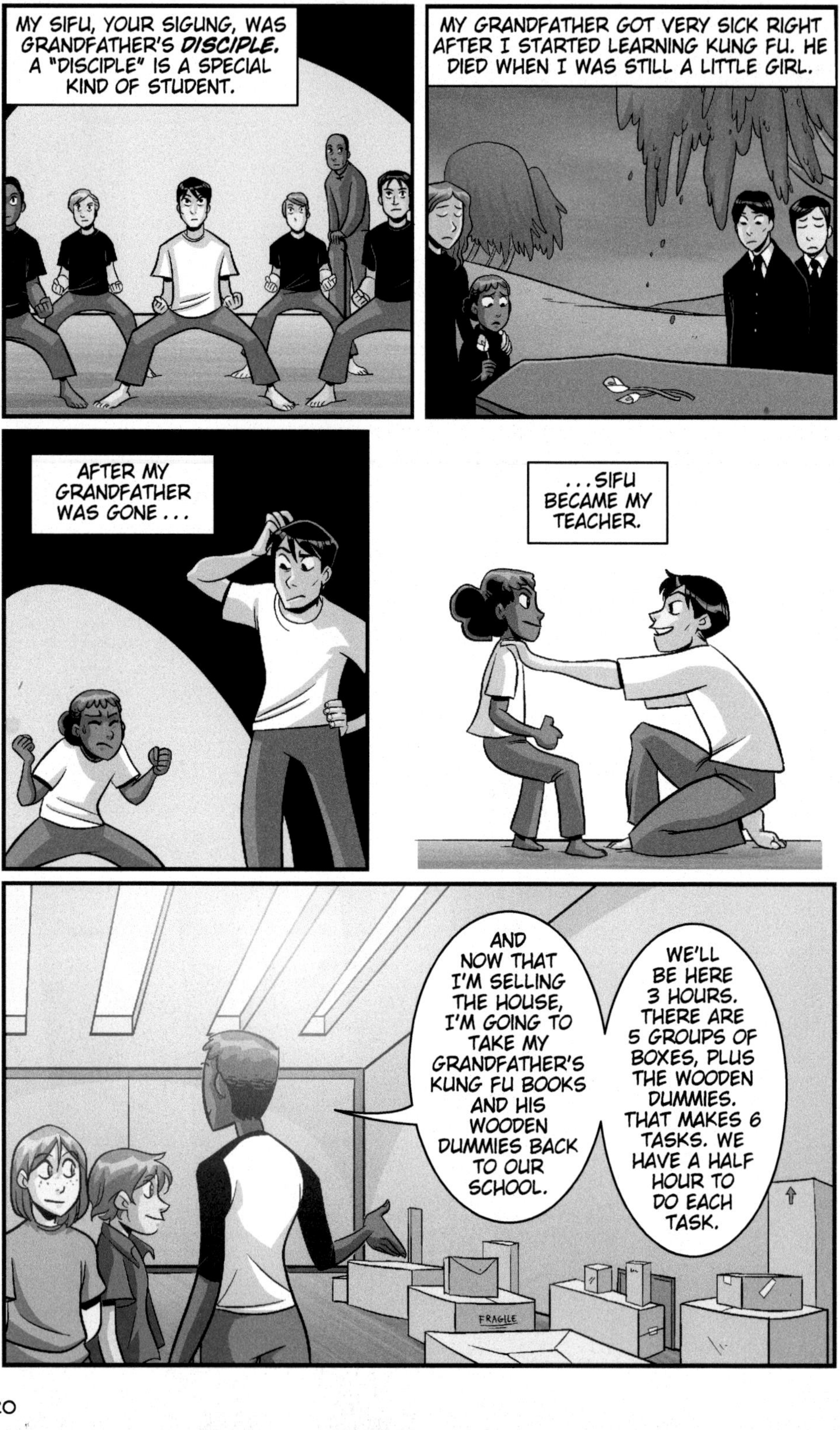
MY SIFU, YOUR SIGUNG, WAS GRANDFATHER'S ***DISCIPLE.*** A "DISCIPLE" IS A SPECIAL KIND OF STUDENT.
MY GRANDFATHER GOT VERY SICK RIGHT AFTER I STARTED LEARNING KUNG FU. HE DIED WHEN I WAS STILL A LITTLE GIRL.
AFTER MY GRANDFATHER WAS GONE . . .
. . . SIFU BECAME MY TEACHER.
AND NOW THAT I'M SELLING THE HOUSE, I'M GOING TO TAKE MY GRANDFATHER'S KUNG FU BOOKS AND HIS WOODEN DUMMIES BACK TO OUR SCHOOL.
WE'LL BE HERE 3 HOURS. THERE ARE 5 GROUPS OF BOXES, PLUS THE WOODEN DUMMIES. THAT MAKES 6 TASKS. WE HAVE A HALF HOUR TO DO EACH TASK.
FRAGILE

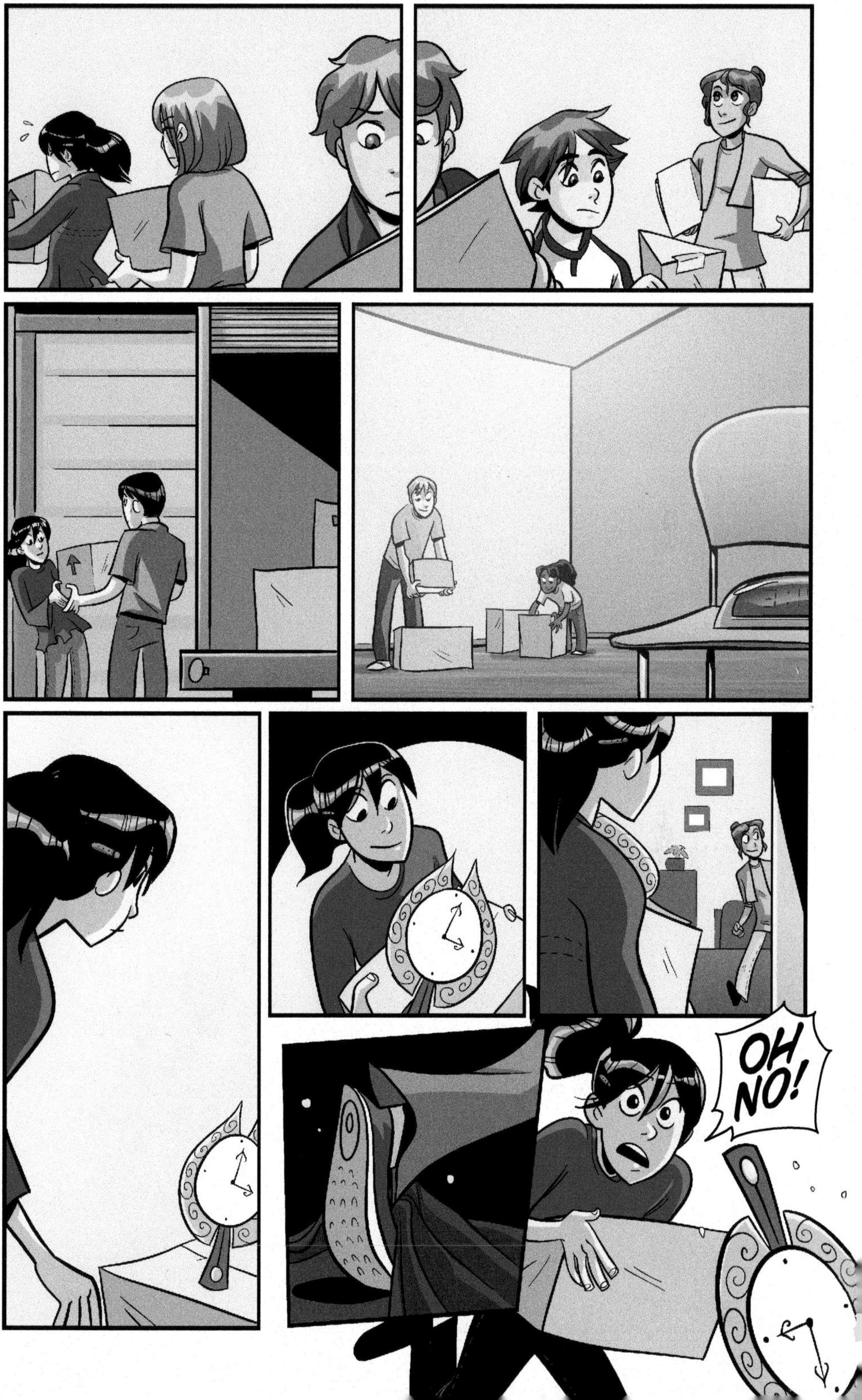
OH NO!

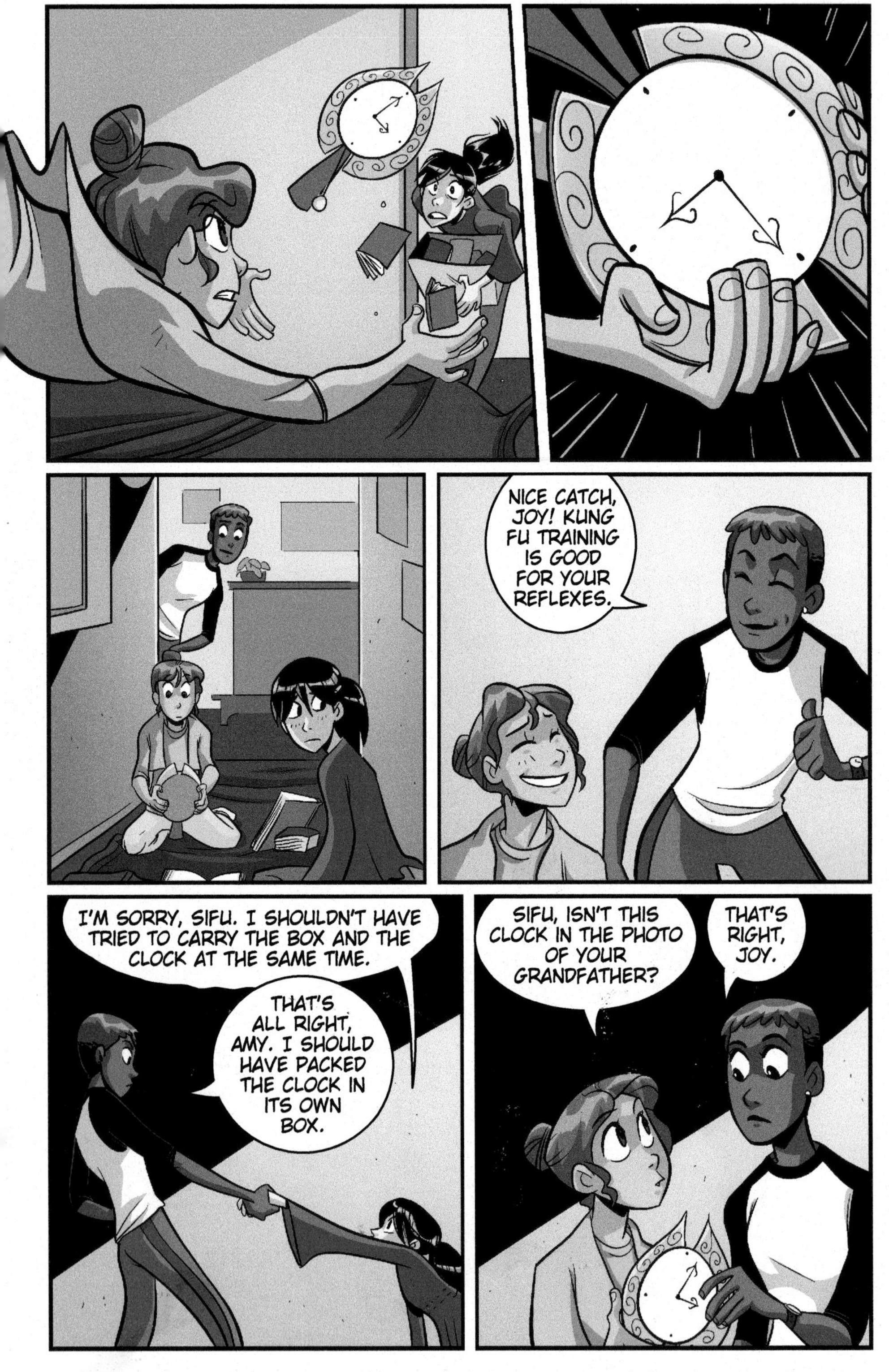
NICE CATCH, JOY! KUNG FU TRAINING IS GOOD FOR YOUR REFLEXES.
I'M SORRY, SIFU. I SHOULDN'T HAVE TRIED TO CARRY THE BOX AND THE CLOCK AT THE SAME TIME.
THAT'S ALL RIGHT, AMY. I SHOULD HAVE PACKED THE CLOCK IN ITS OWN BOX.
SIFU, ISN'T THIS CLOCK IN THE PHOTO OF YOUR GRANDFATHER?
THAT'S RIGHT, JOY.

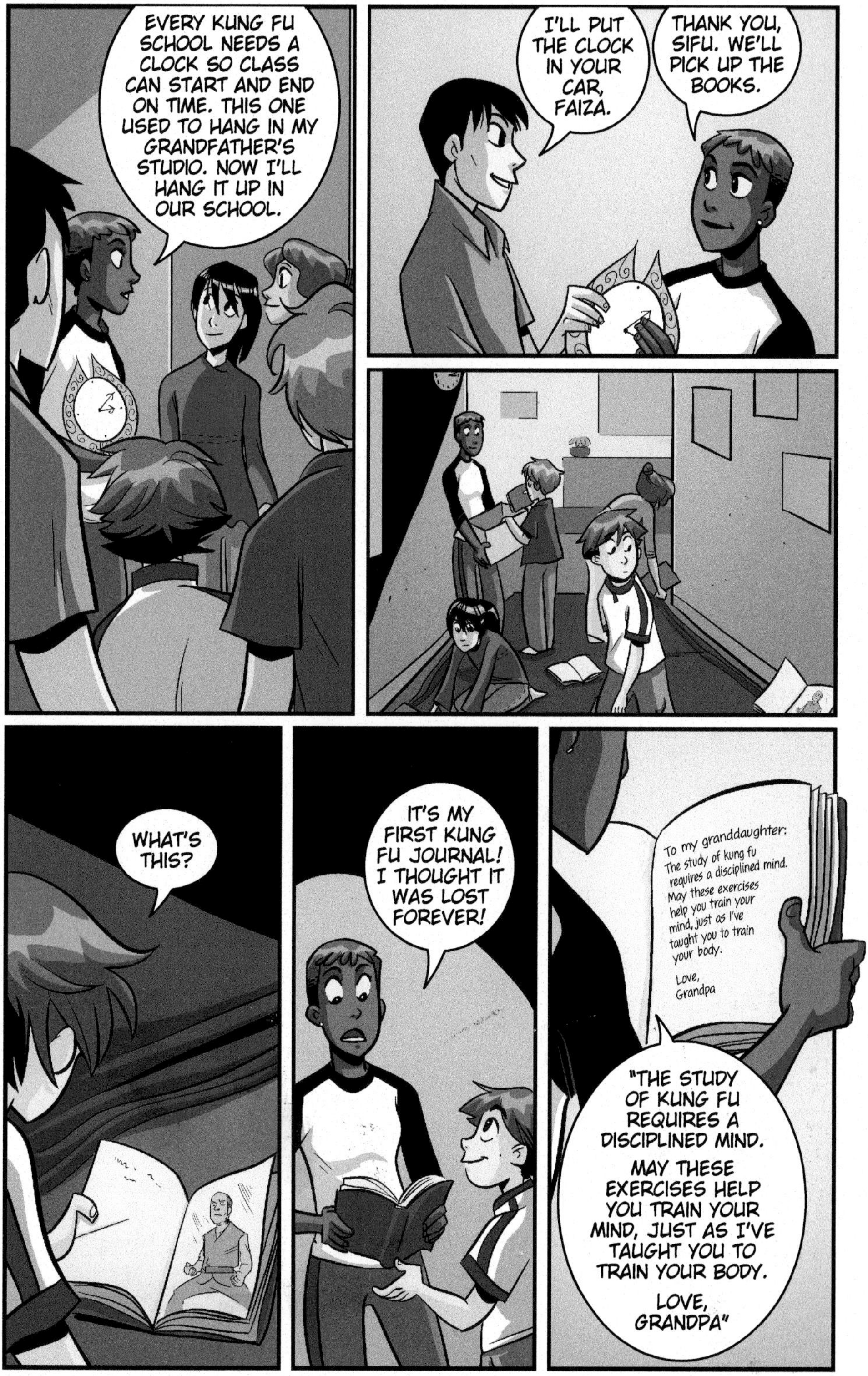
EVERY KUNG FU SCHOOL NEEDS A CLOCK SO CLASS CAN START AND END ON TIME. THIS ONE USED TO HANG IN MY GRANDFATHER'S STUDIO. NOW I'LL HANG IT UP IN OUR SCHOOL.
I'LL PUT THE CLOCK IN YOUR CAR, FAIZA.
THANK YOU, SIFU. WE'LL PICK UP THE BOOKS.
WHAT'S THIS?
IT'S MY FIRST KUNG FU JOURNAL! I THOUGHT IT WAS LOST FOREVER!
To my granddaughter: The study of kung fu requires a disciplined mind. May these exercises help you train your mind, just as I've taught you to train your body.
Love, Grandpa
"THE STUDY OF KUNG FU REQUIRES A DISCIPLINED MIND.
MAY THESE EXERCISES HELP YOU TRAIN YOUR MIND, JUST AS I'VE TAUGHT YOU TO TRAIN YOUR BODY.
LOVE, GRANDPA"

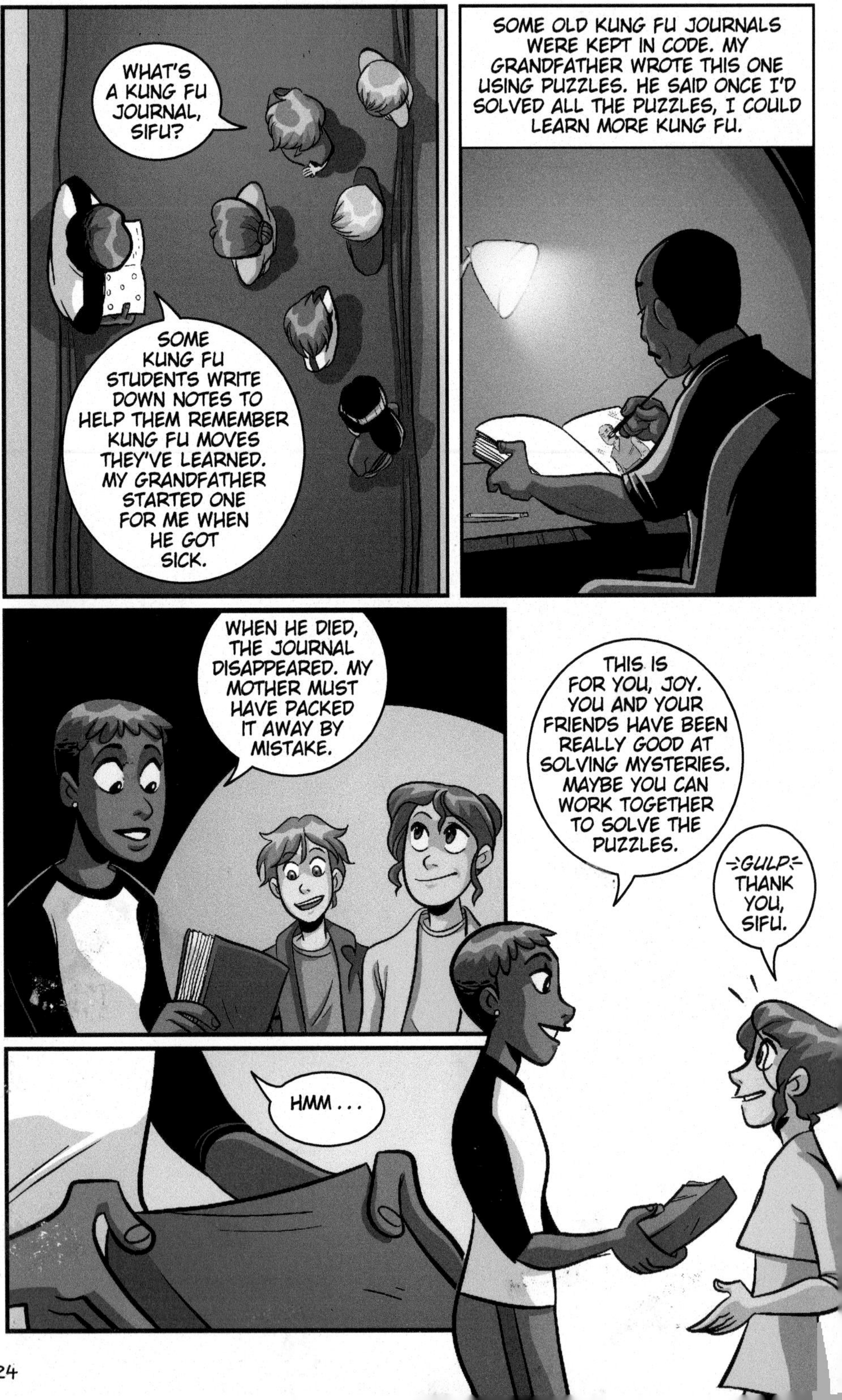
WHAT'S A KUNG FU JOURNAL, SIFU?
SOME KUNG FU STUDENTS WRITE DOWN NOTES TO HELP THEM REMEMBER KUNG FU MOVES THEY'VE LEARNED. MY GRANDFATHER STARTED ONE FOR ME WHEN HE GOT SICK.
SOME OLD KUNG FU JOURNALS WERE KEPT IN CODE. MY GRANDFATHER WROTE THIS ONE USING PUZZLES. HE SAID ONCE I'D SOLVED ALL THE PUZZLES, I COULD LEARN MORE KUNG FU.
WHEN HE DIED, THE JOURNAL DISAPPEARED. MY MOTHER MUST HAVE PACKED IT AWAY BY MISTAKE.
HMM . . .
THIS IS FOR YOU, JOY. YOU AND YOUR FRIENDS HAVE BEEN REALLY GOOD AT SOLVING MYSTERIES. MAYBE YOU CAN WORK TOGETHER TO SOLVE THE PUZZLES.
GULP
THANK YOU, SIFU.

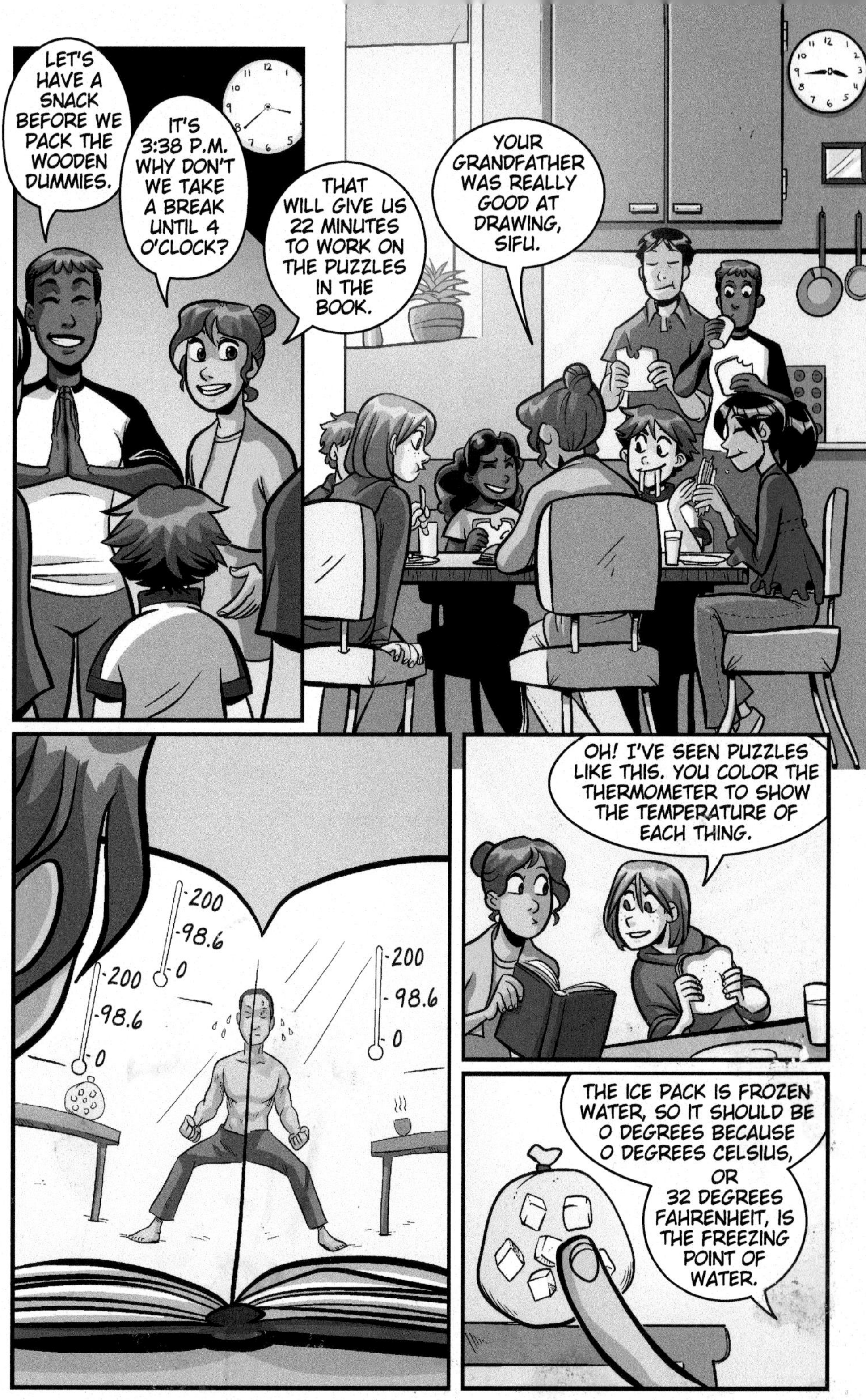
LET'S HAVE A SNACK BEFORE WE PACK THE WOODEN DUMMIES.
IT'S 3:38 P.M. WHY DON'T WE TAKE A BREAK UNTIL 4 O'CLOCK?
THAT WILL GIVE US 22 MINUTES TO WORK ON THE PUZZLES IN THE BOOK.
YOUR GRANDFATHER WAS REALLY GOOD AT DRAWING, SIFU.
200
98.6
0
200
98.6
0
200
98.6
0
OH! I'VE SEEN PUZZLES LIKE THIS. YOU COLOR THE THERMOMETER TO SHOW THE TEMPERATURE OF EACH THING.
THE ICE PACK IS FROZEN WATER, SO IT SHOULD BE 0 DEGREES BECAUSE 0 DEGREES CELSIUS, OR 32 DEGREES FAHRENHEIT, IS THE FREEZING POINT OF WATER.

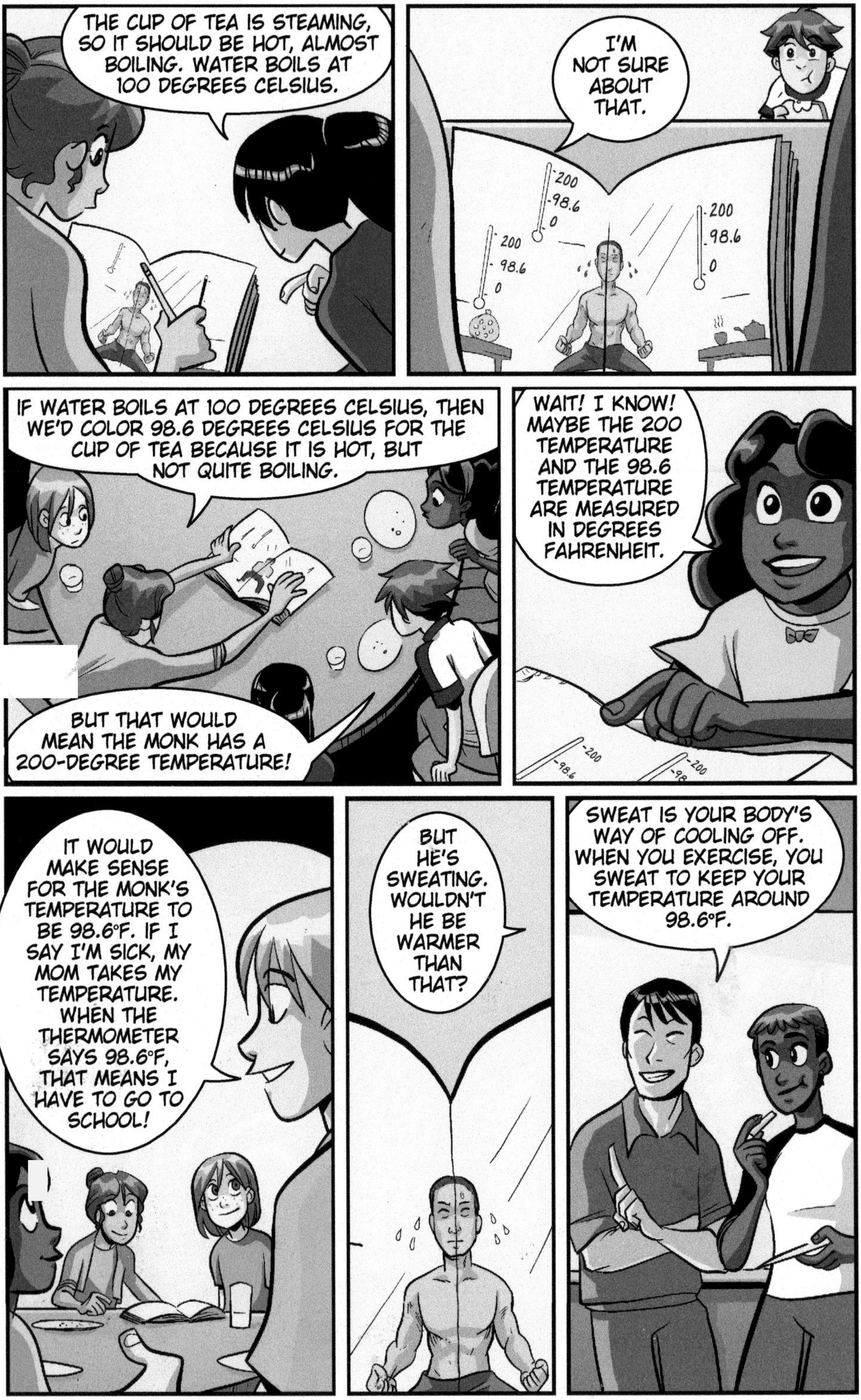
THE CUP OF TEA IS STEAMING, SO IT SHOULD BE HOT, ALMOST BOILING. WATER BOILS AT 100 DEGREES CELSIUS.
I'M NOT SURE ABOUT THAT.
200
98.6
0
200
98.6
0
200
98.6
0
IF WATER BOILS AT 100 DEGREES CELSIUS, THEN WE'D COLOR 98.6 DEGREES CELSIUS FOR THE CUP OF TEA BECAUSE IT IS HOT, BUT NOT QUITE BOILING.
BUT THAT WOULD MEAN THE MONK HAS A 200-DEGREE TEMPERATURE!
WAIT! I KNOW! MAYBE THE 200 TEMPERATURE AND THE 98.6 TEMPERATURE ARE MEASURED IN DEGREES FAHRENHEIT.
IT WOULD MAKE SENSE FOR THE MONK'S TEMPERATURE TO BE 98.6°F. IF I SAY I'M SICK, MY MOM TAKES MY TEMPERATURE. WHEN THE THERMOMETER SAYS 98.6°F, THAT MEANS I HAVE TO GO TO SCHOOL!
BUT HE'S SWEATING. WOULDN'T HE BE WARMER THAN THAT?
SWEAT IS YOUR BODY'S WAY OF COOLING OFF. WHEN YOU EXERCISE, YOU SWEAT TO KEEP YOUR TEMPERATURE AROUND 98.6°F.

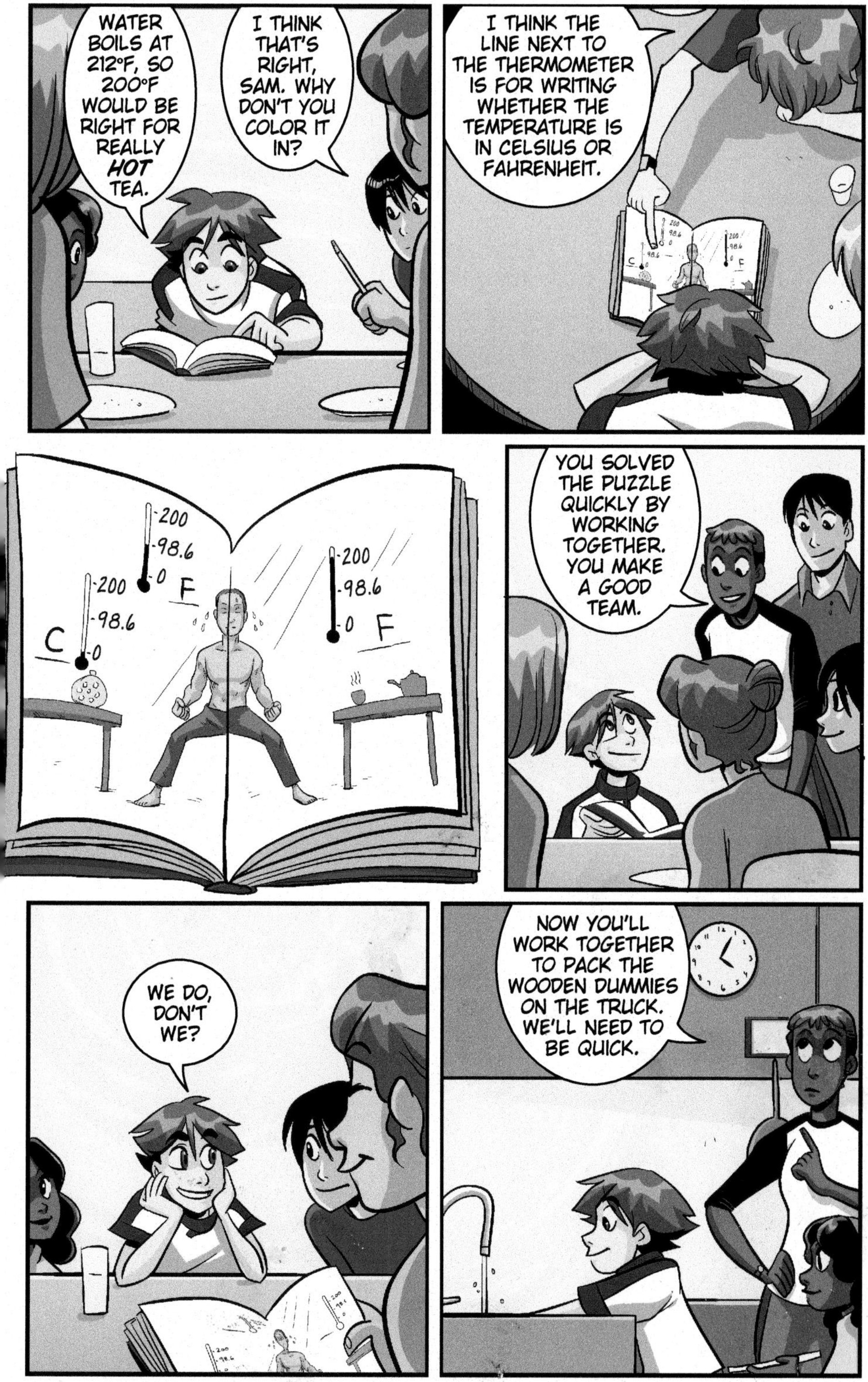
WATER BOILS AT 212°F, SO 200°F WOULD BE RIGHT FOR REALLY *HOT* TEA.
I THINK THAT'S RIGHT, SAM. WHY DON'T YOU COLOR IT IN?
I THINK THE LINE NEXT TO THE THERMOMETER IS FOR WRITING WHETHER THE TEMPERATURE IS IN CELSIUS OR FAHRENHEIT.
200
98.6
0
F
200
98.6
0
C
200
98.6
0
F
YOU SOLVED THE PUZZLE QUICKLY BY WORKING TOGETHER. YOU MAKE A GOOD TEAM.
WE DO, DON'T WE?
NOW YOU'LL WORK TOGETHER TO PACK THE WOODEN DUMMIES ON THE TRUCK. WE'LL NEED TO BE QUICK.

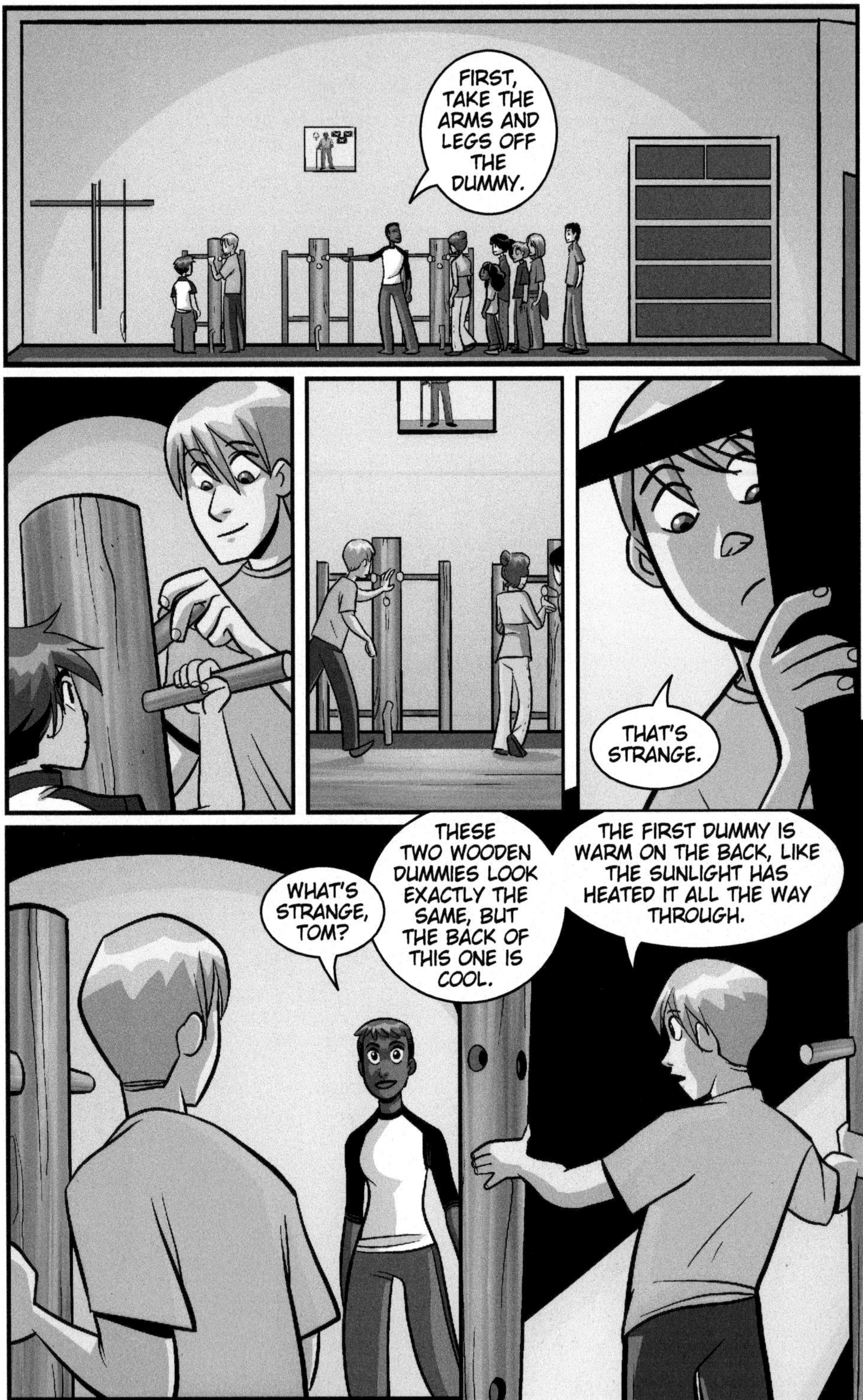

FIRST, TAKE THE ARMS AND LEGS OFF THE DUMMY.
THAT'S STRANGE.
WHAT'S STRANGE, TOM?
THESE TWO WOODEN DUMMIES LOOK EXACTLY THE SAME, BUT THE BACK OF THIS ONE IS COOL.
THE FIRST DUMMY IS WARM ON THE BACK, LIKE THE SUNLIGHT HAS HEATED IT ALL THE WAY THROUGH.

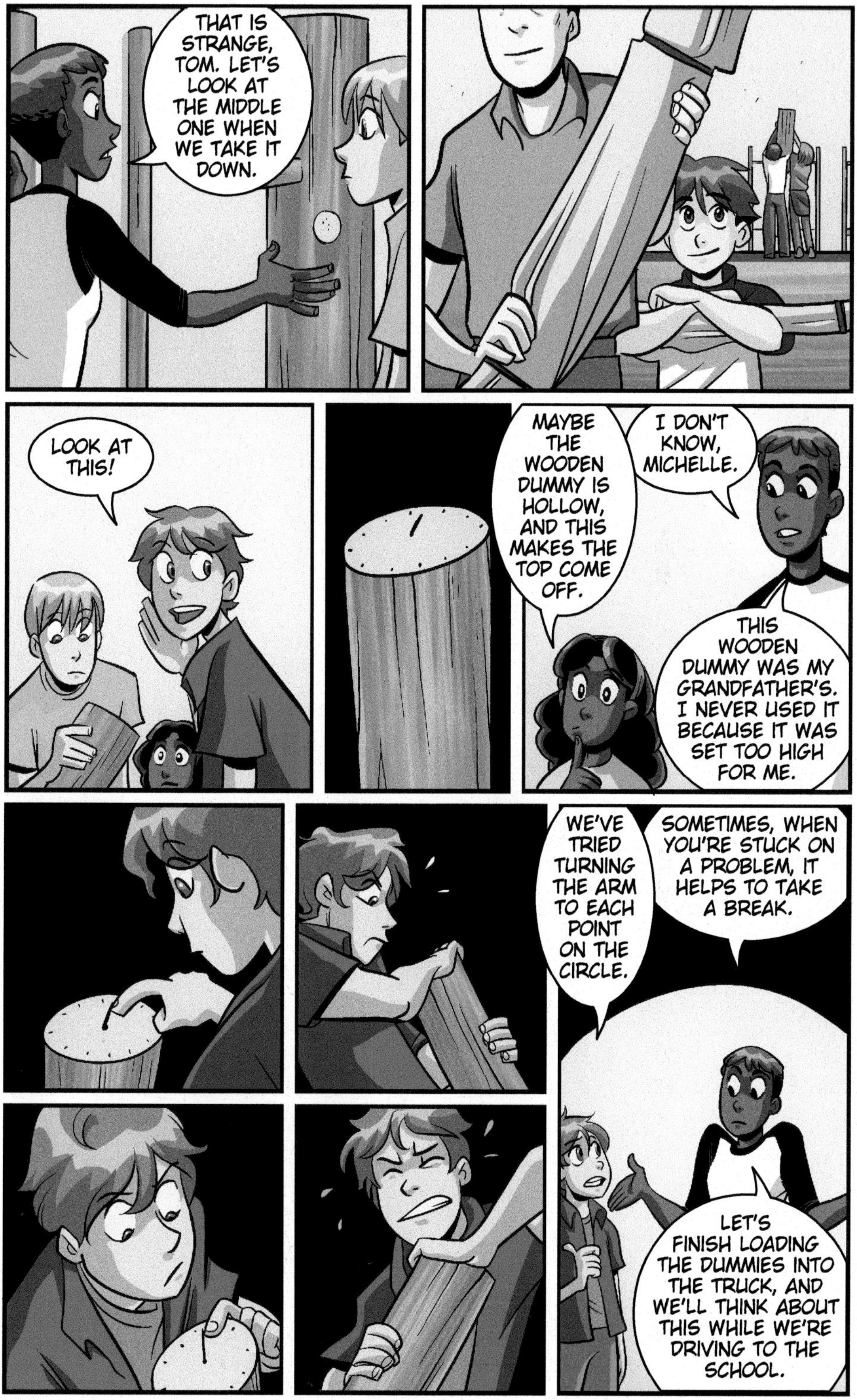
THAT IS STRANGE, TOM. LET'S LOOK AT THE MIDDLE ONE WHEN WE TAKE IT DOWN.
LOOK AT THIS!
MAYBE THE WOODEN DUMMY IS HOLLOW, AND THIS MAKES THE TOP COME OFF.
I DON'T KNOW, MICHELLE.
THIS WOODEN DUMMY WAS MY GRANDFATHER'S. I NEVER USED IT BECAUSE IT WAS SET TOO HIGH FOR ME.
WE'VE TRIED TURNING THE ARM TO EACH POINT ON THE CIRCLE.
SOMETIMES, WHEN YOU'RE STUCK ON A PROBLEM, IT HELPS TO TAKE A BREAK.
LET'S FINISH LOADING THE DUMMIES INTO THE TRUCK, AND WE'LL THINK ABOUT THIS WHILE WE'RE DRIVING TO THE SCHOOL.

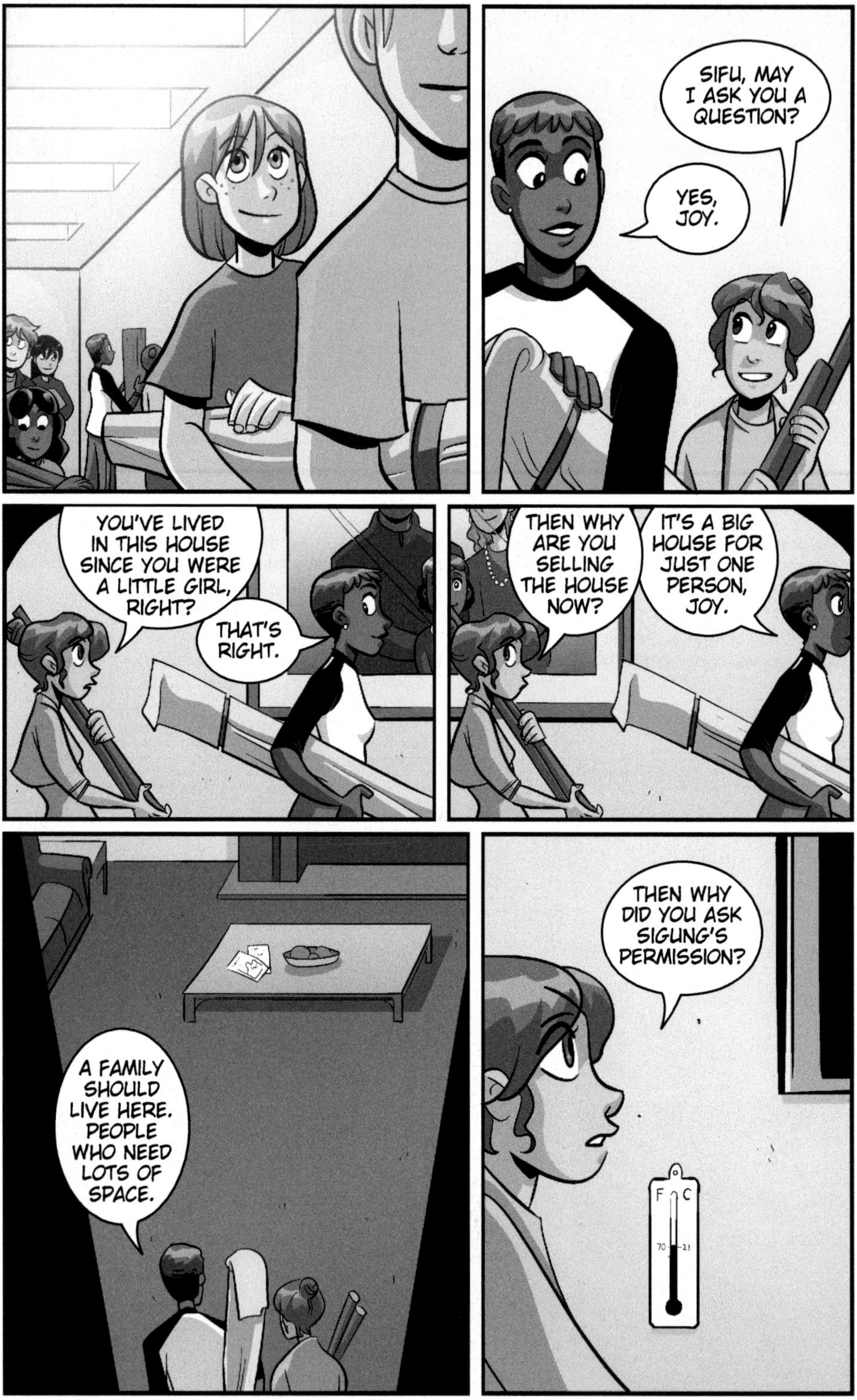
SIFU, MAY I ASK YOU A QUESTION?
YES, JOY.
YOU'VE LIVED IN THIS HOUSE SINCE YOU WERE A LITTLE GIRL, RIGHT?
THAT'S RIGHT.
THEN WHY ARE YOU SELLING THE HOUSE NOW?
IT'S A BIG HOUSE FOR JUST ONE PERSON, JOY.
A FAMILY SHOULD LIVE HERE. PEOPLE WHO NEED LOTS OF SPACE.
THEN WHY DID YOU ASK SIGUNG'S PERMISSION?

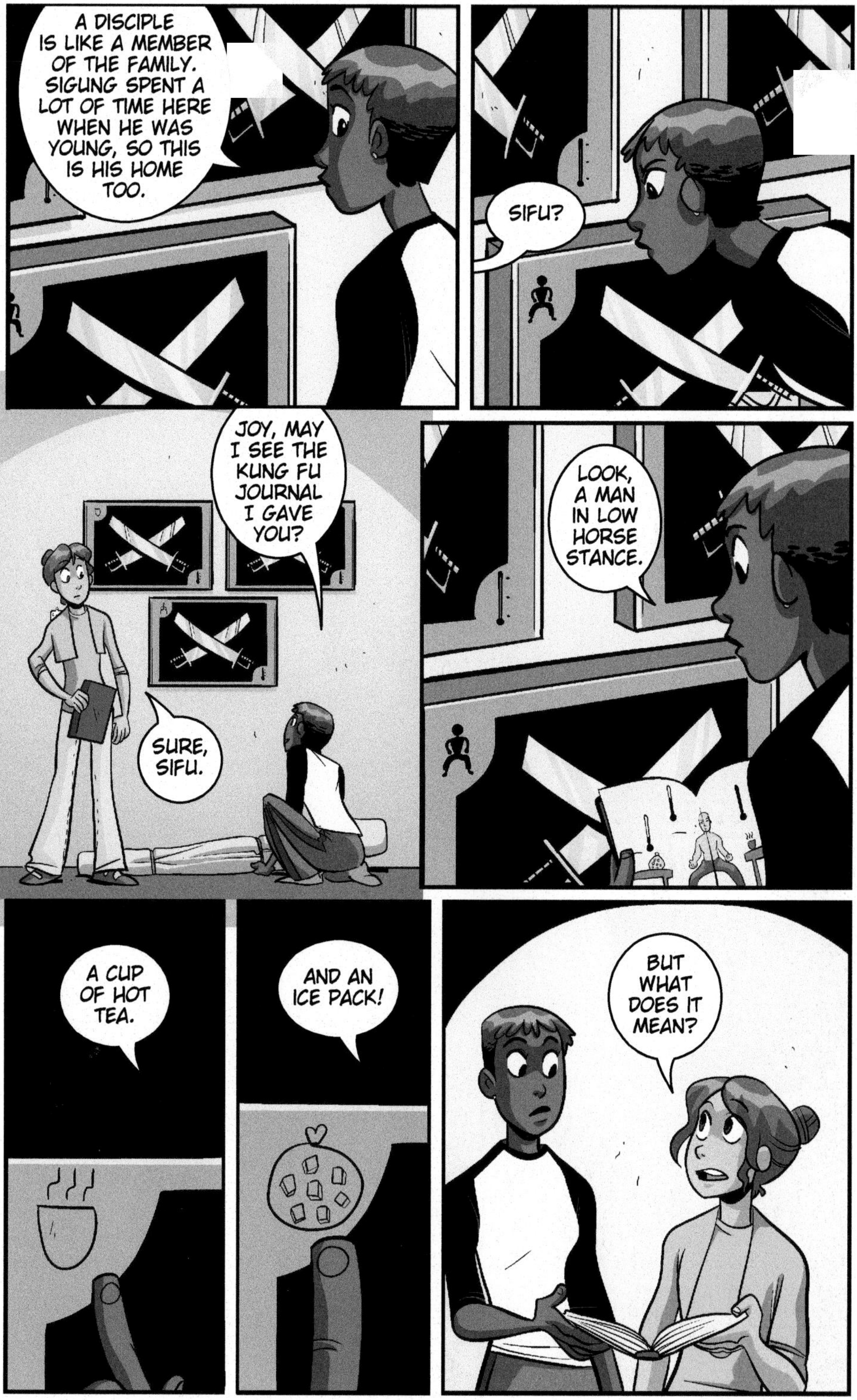
A DISCIPLE IS LIKE A MEMBER OF THE FAMILY. SIGUNG SPENT A LOT OF TIME HERE WHEN HE WAS YOUNG, SO THIS IS HIS HOME TOO.
SIFU?
JOY, MAY I SEE THE KUNG FU JOURNAL I GAVE YOU?
SURE, SIFU.
LOOK, A MAN IN LOW HORSE STANCE.
A CUP OF HOT TEA.
AND AN ICE PACK!
BUT WHAT DOES IT MEAN?

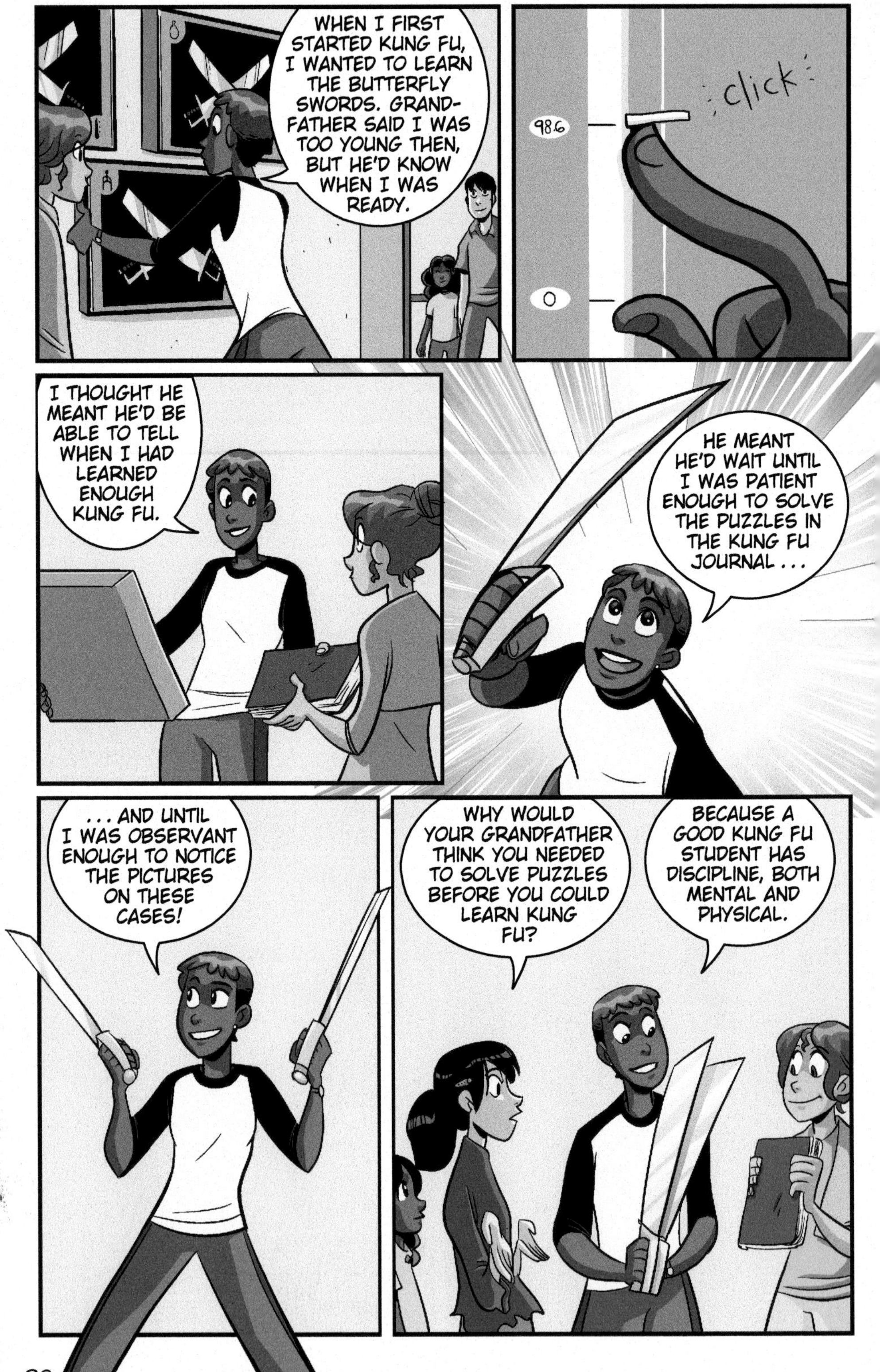

WHEN I FIRST STARTED KUNG FU, I WANTED TO LEARN THE BUTTERFLY SWORDS. GRAND-FATHER SAID I WAS TOO YOUNG THEN, BUT HE'D KNOW WHEN I WAS READY.
98.6
click
0
I THOUGHT HE MEANT HE'D BE ABLE TO TELL WHEN I HAD LEARNED ENOUGH KUNG FU.
HE MEANT HE'D WAIT UNTIL I WAS PATIENT ENOUGH TO SOLVE THE PUZZLES IN THE KUNG FU JOURNAL . . .
. . . AND UNTIL I WAS OBSERVANT ENOUGH TO NOTICE THE PICTURES ON THESE CASES!
WHY WOULD YOUR GRANDFATHER THINK YOU NEEDED TO SOLVE PUZZLES BEFORE YOU COULD LEARN KUNG FU?
BECAUSE A GOOD KUNG FU STUDENT HAS DISCIPLINE, BOTH MENTAL AND PHYSICAL.

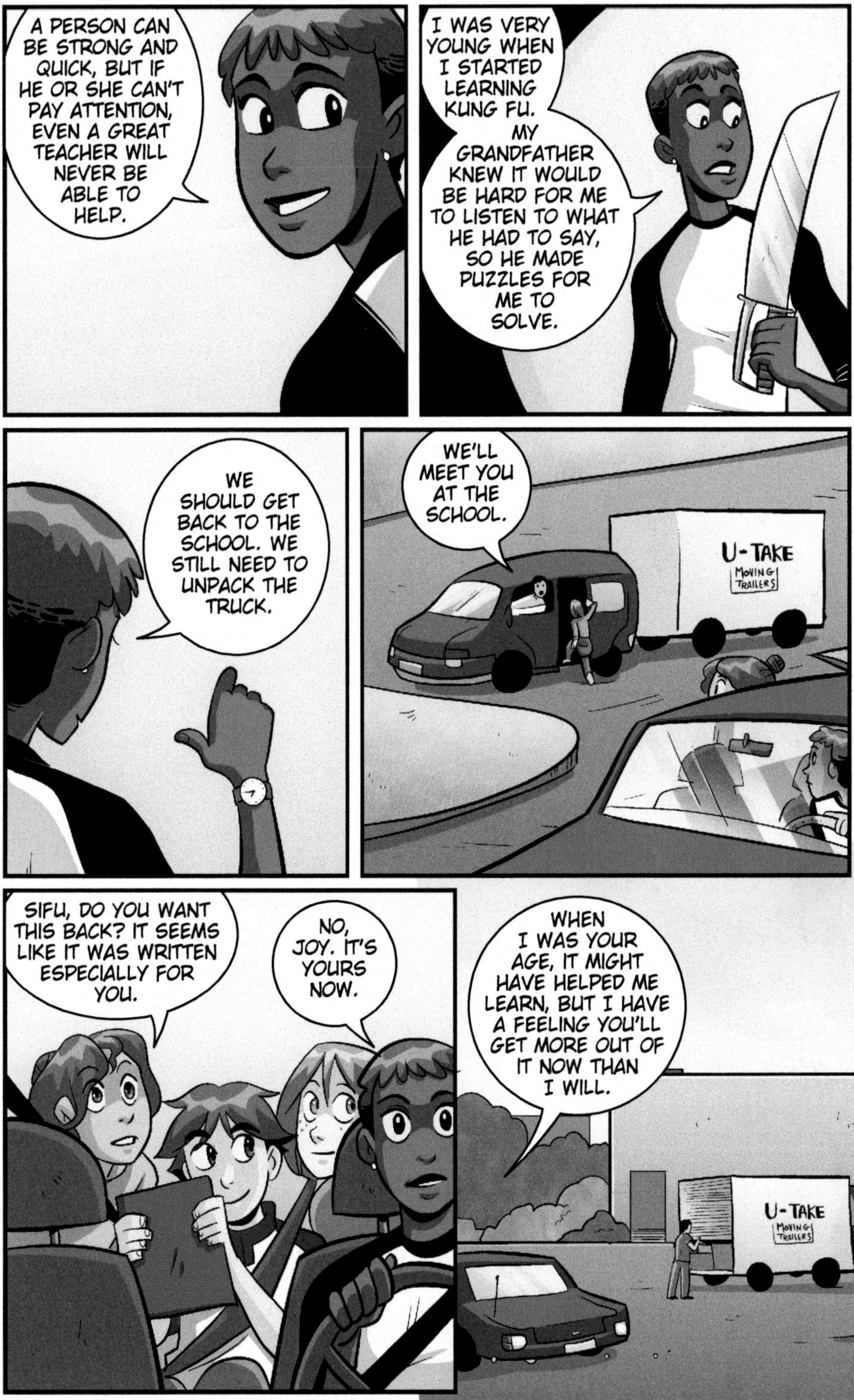
A PERSON CAN BE STRONG AND QUICK, BUT IF HE OR SHE CAN'T PAY ATTENTION, EVEN A GREAT TEACHER WILL NEVER BE ABLE TO HELP.
I WAS VERY YOUNG WHEN I STARTED LEARNING KUNG FU.
MY GRANDFATHER KNEW IT WOULD BE HARD FOR ME TO LISTEN TO WHAT HE HAD TO SAY, SO HE MADE PUZZLES FOR ME TO SOLVE.
WE SHOULD GET BACK TO THE SCHOOL. WE STILL NEED TO UNPACK THE TRUCK.
WE'LL MEET YOU AT THE SCHOOL.
U-TAKE
MOVING TRAILERS
SIFU, DO YOU WANT THIS BACK? IT SEEMS LIKE IT WAS WRITTEN ESPECIALLY FOR YOU.
NO, JOY. IT'S YOURS NOW.
WHEN I WAS YOUR AGE, IT MIGHT HAVE HELPED ME LEARN, BUT I HAVE A FEELING YOU'LL GET MORE OUT OF IT NOW THAN I WILL.
U-TAKE
MOVING TRAILERS

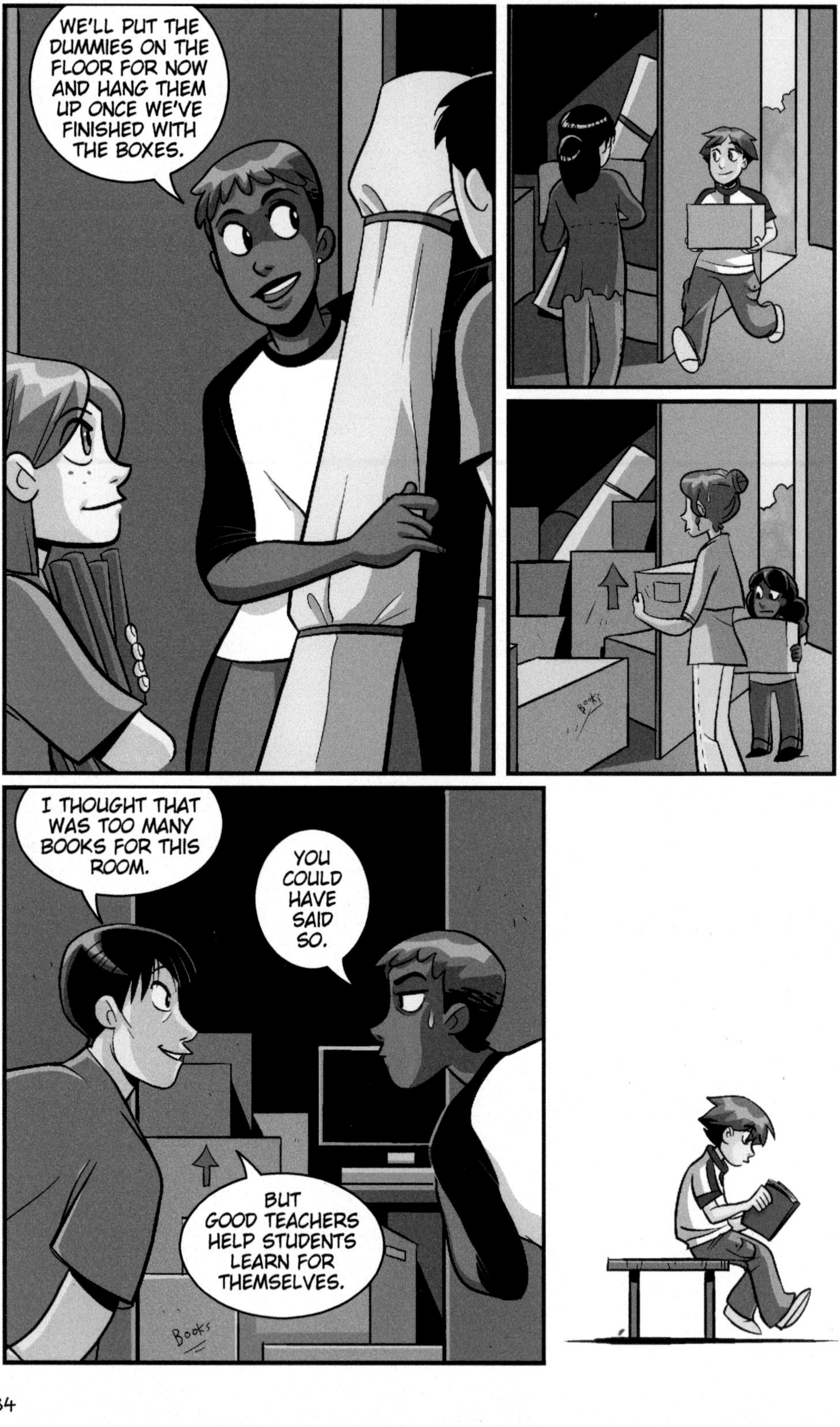
WE'LL PUT THE DUMMIES ON THE FLOOR FOR NOW AND HANG THEM UP ONCE WE'VE FINISHED WITH THE BOXES.
I THOUGHT THAT WAS TOO MANY BOOKS FOR THIS ROOM.
YOU COULD HAVE SAID SO.
BUT GOOD TEACHERS HELP STUDENTS LEARN FOR THEMSELVES.
Books

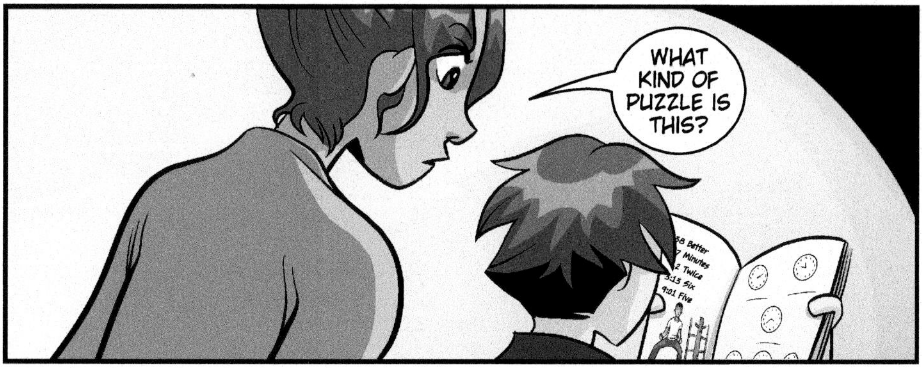
WHAT KIND OF PUZZLE IS THIS?

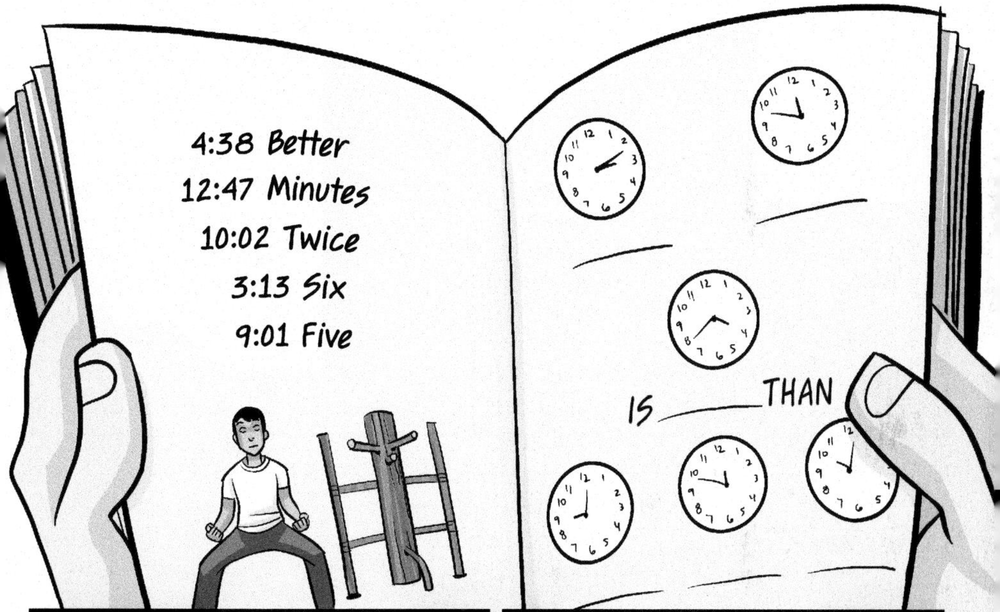
4:38 Better
12:47 Minutes
10:02 Twice
3:13 Six
9:01 Five
IS _____ THAN

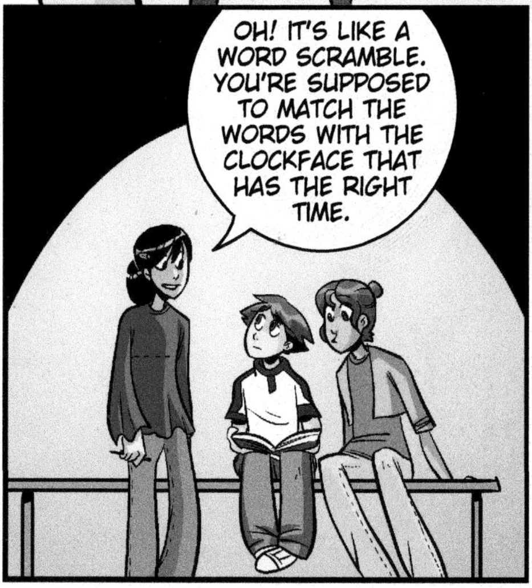
OH! IT'S LIKE A WORD SCRAMBLE. YOU'RE SUPPOSED TO MATCH THE WORDS WITH THE CLOCKFACE THAT HAS THE RIGHT TIME.

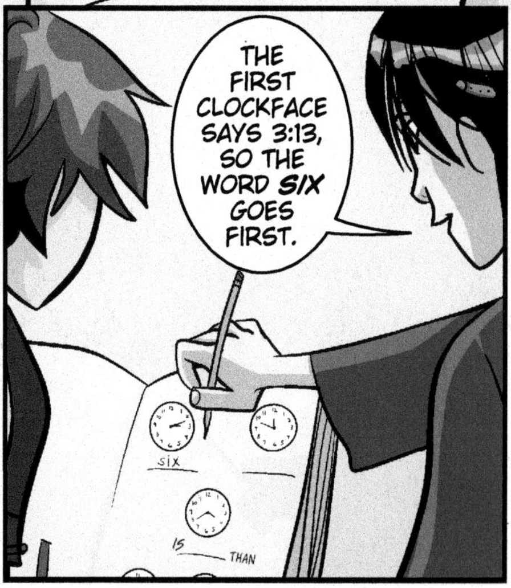
THE FIRST CLOCKFACE SAYS 3:13, SO THE WORD ***SIX*** GOES FIRST.
SIX
IS _____ THAN

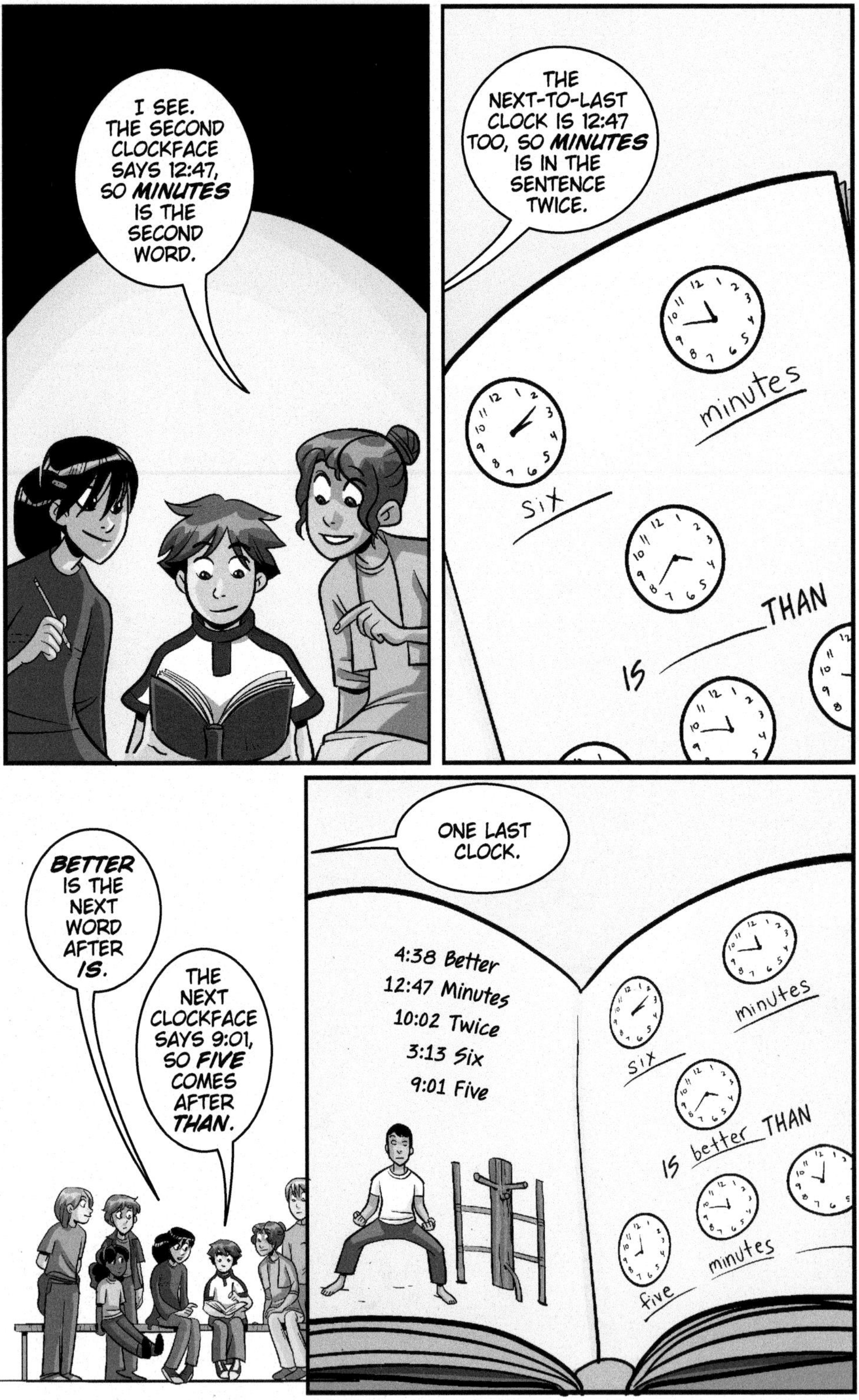
I SEE. THE SECOND CLOCKFACE SAYS 12:47, SO ***MINUTES*** IS THE SECOND WORD.
THE NEXT-TO-LAST CLOCK IS 12:47 TOO, SO ***MINUTES*** IS IN THE SENTENCE TWICE.
six
minutes
IS
THAN
BETTER IS THE NEXT WORD AFTER ***IS***.
THE NEXT CLOCKFACE SAYS 9:01, SO ***FIVE*** COMES AFTER ***THAN***.
ONE LAST CLOCK.
4:38 Better
12:47 Minutes
10:02 Twice
3:13 Six
9:01 Five
six
minutes
IS better THAN
five minutes

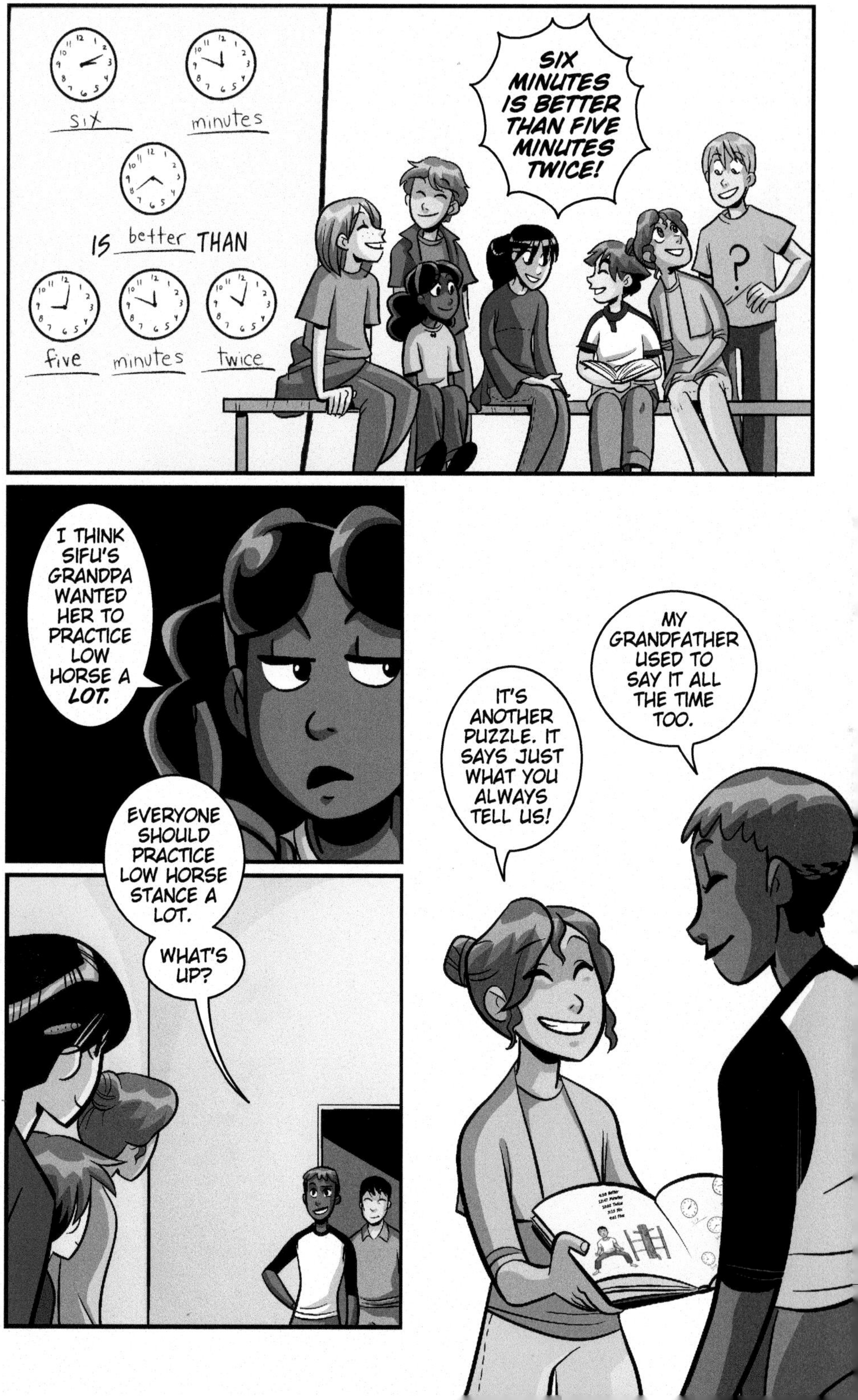
six
minutes
IS better THAN
five
minutes
twice
SIX MINUTES IS BETTER THAN FIVE MINUTES TWICE!
I THINK SIFU'S GRANDPA WANTED HER TO PRACTICE LOW HORSE A *LOT.*
EVERYONE SHOULD PRACTICE LOW HORSE STANCE A LOT.
WHAT'S UP?
IT'S ANOTHER PUZZLE. IT SAYS JUST WHAT YOU ALWAYS TELL US!
MY GRANDFATHER USED TO SAY IT ALL THE TIME TOO.

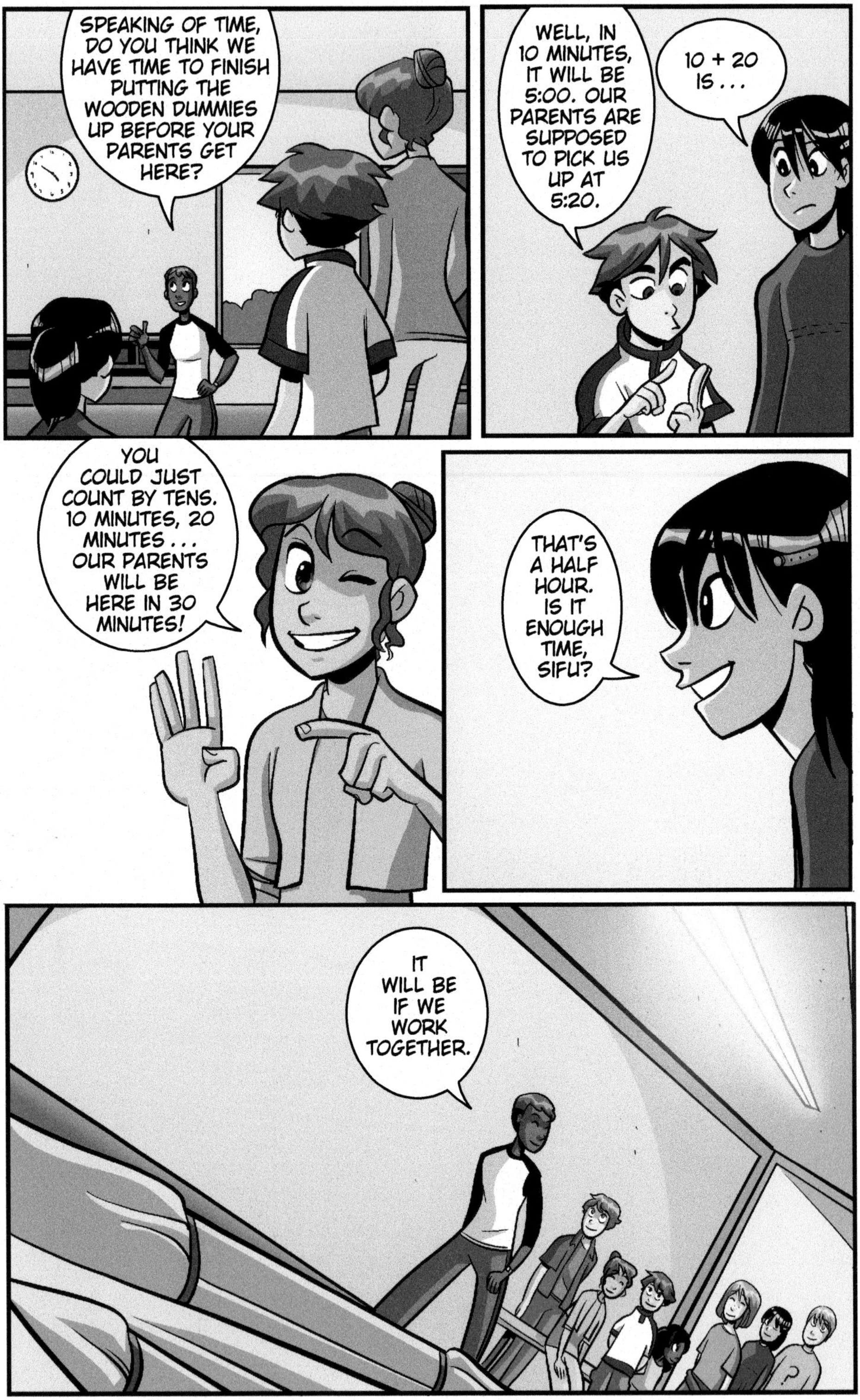

SPEAKING OF TIME, DO YOU THINK WE HAVE TIME TO FINISH PUTTING THE WOODEN DUMMIES UP BEFORE YOUR PARENTS GET HERE?
WELL, IN 10 MINUTES, IT WILL BE 5:00. OUR PARENTS ARE SUPPOSED TO PICK US UP AT 5:20.
10 + 20 IS . . .
YOU COULD JUST COUNT BY TENS. 10 MINUTES, 20 MINUTES . . . OUR PARENTS WILL BE HERE IN 30 MINUTES!
THAT'S A HALF HOUR. IS IT ENOUGH TIME, SIFU?
IT WILL BE IF WE WORK TOGETHER.

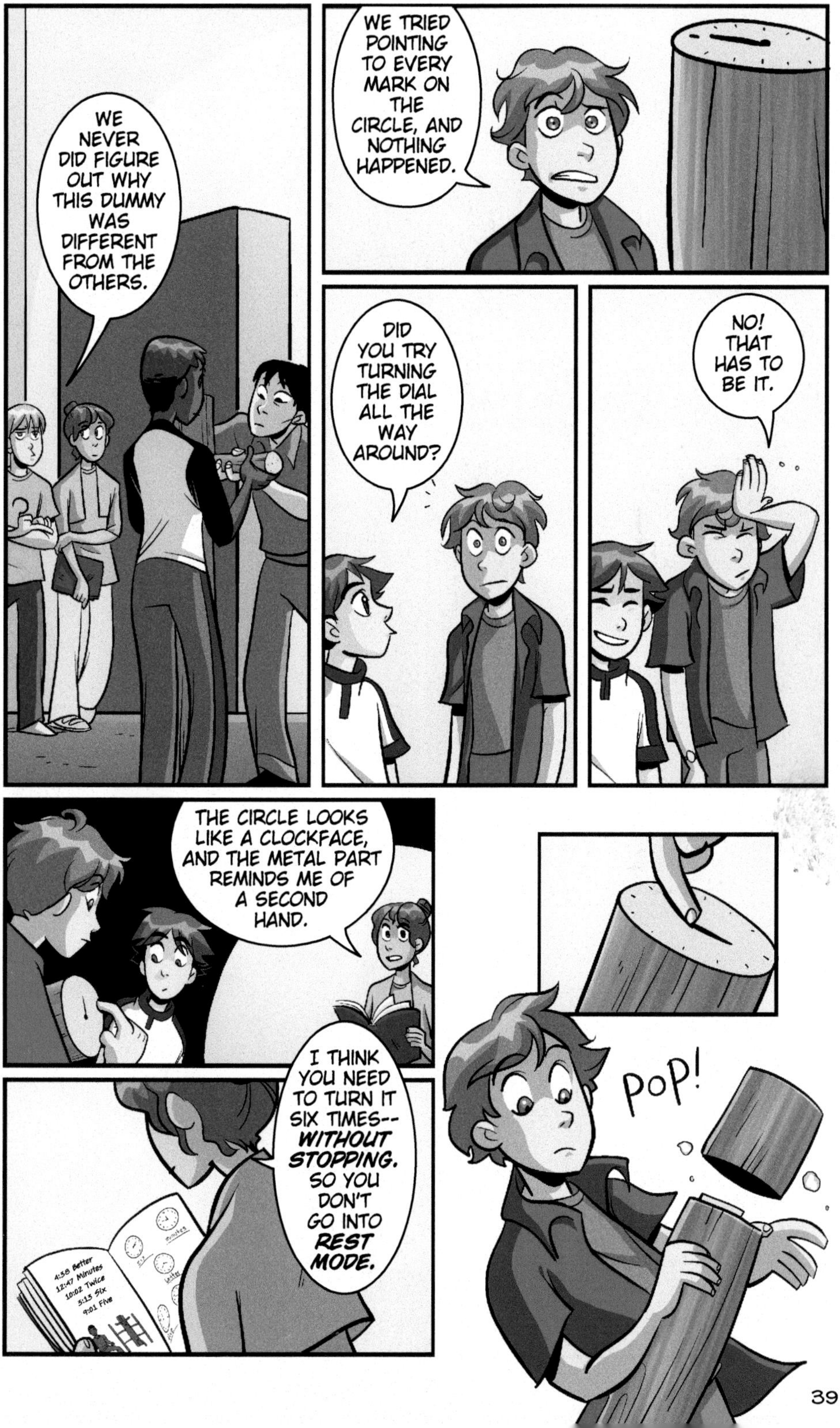
WE NEVER DID FIGURE OUT WHY THIS DUMMY WAS DIFFERENT FROM THE OTHERS.
WE TRIED POINTING TO EVERY MARK ON THE CIRCLE, AND NOTHING HAPPENED.
DID YOU TRY TURNING THE DIAL ALL THE WAY AROUND?
NO! THAT HAS TO BE IT.
THE CIRCLE LOOKS LIKE A CLOCKFACE, AND THE METAL PART REMINDS ME OF A SECOND HAND.
I THINK YOU NEED TO TURN IT SIX TIMES-- ***WITHOUT STOPPING.*** SO YOU DON'T GO INTO ***REST MODE.***
4:38 Better
12:47 Minutes
10:02 Twice
3:15 Six
9:01 Five
POP!

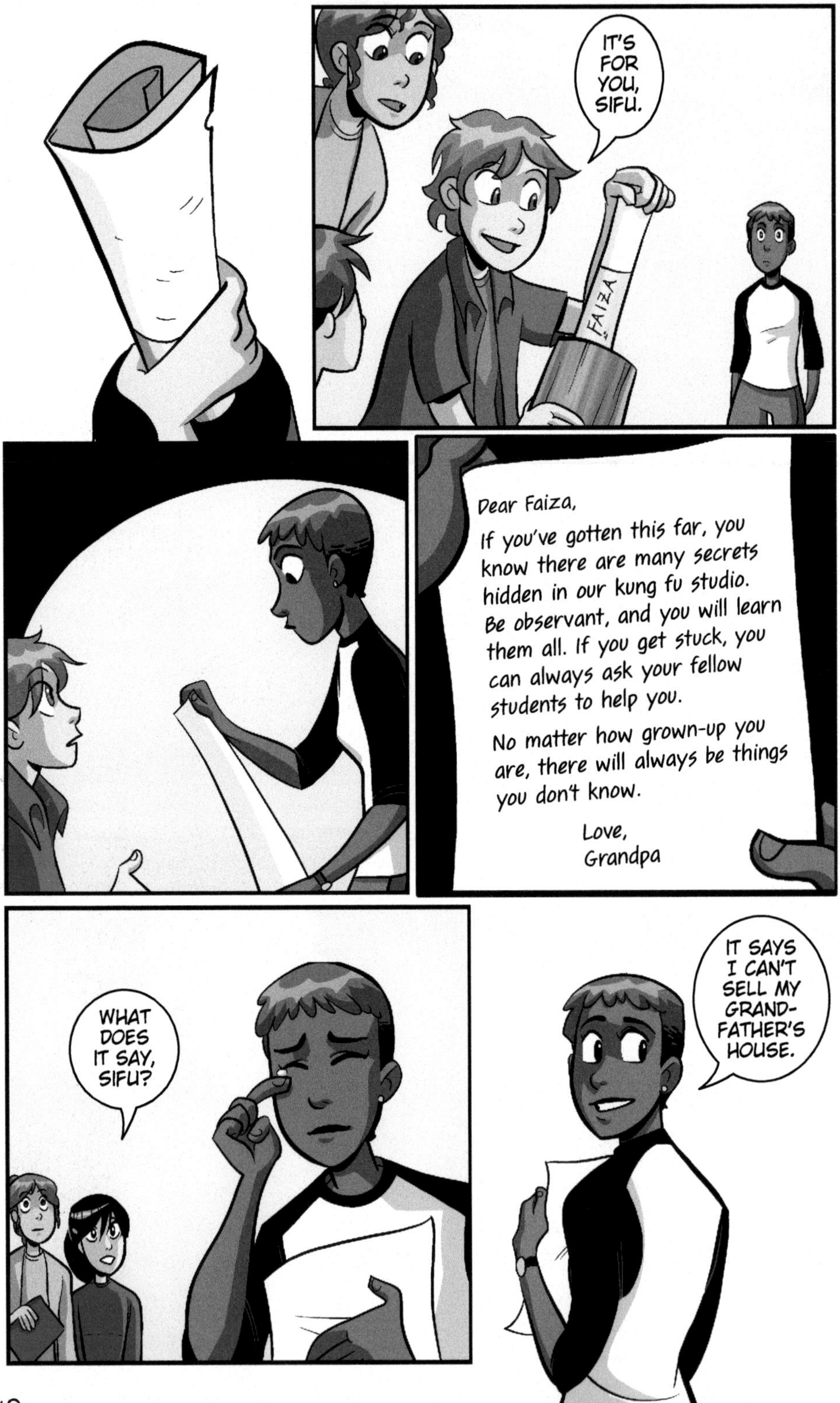
IT'S FOR YOU, SIFU.
FAIZA
Dear Faiza,
If you've gotten this far, you know there are many secrets hidden in our kung fu studio. Be observant, and you will learn them all. If you get stuck, you can always ask your fellow students to help you.
No matter how grown-up you are, there will always be things you don't know.
Love,
Grandpa
WHAT DOES IT SAY, SIFU?
IT SAYS I CAN'T SELL MY GRAND-FATHER'S HOUSE.

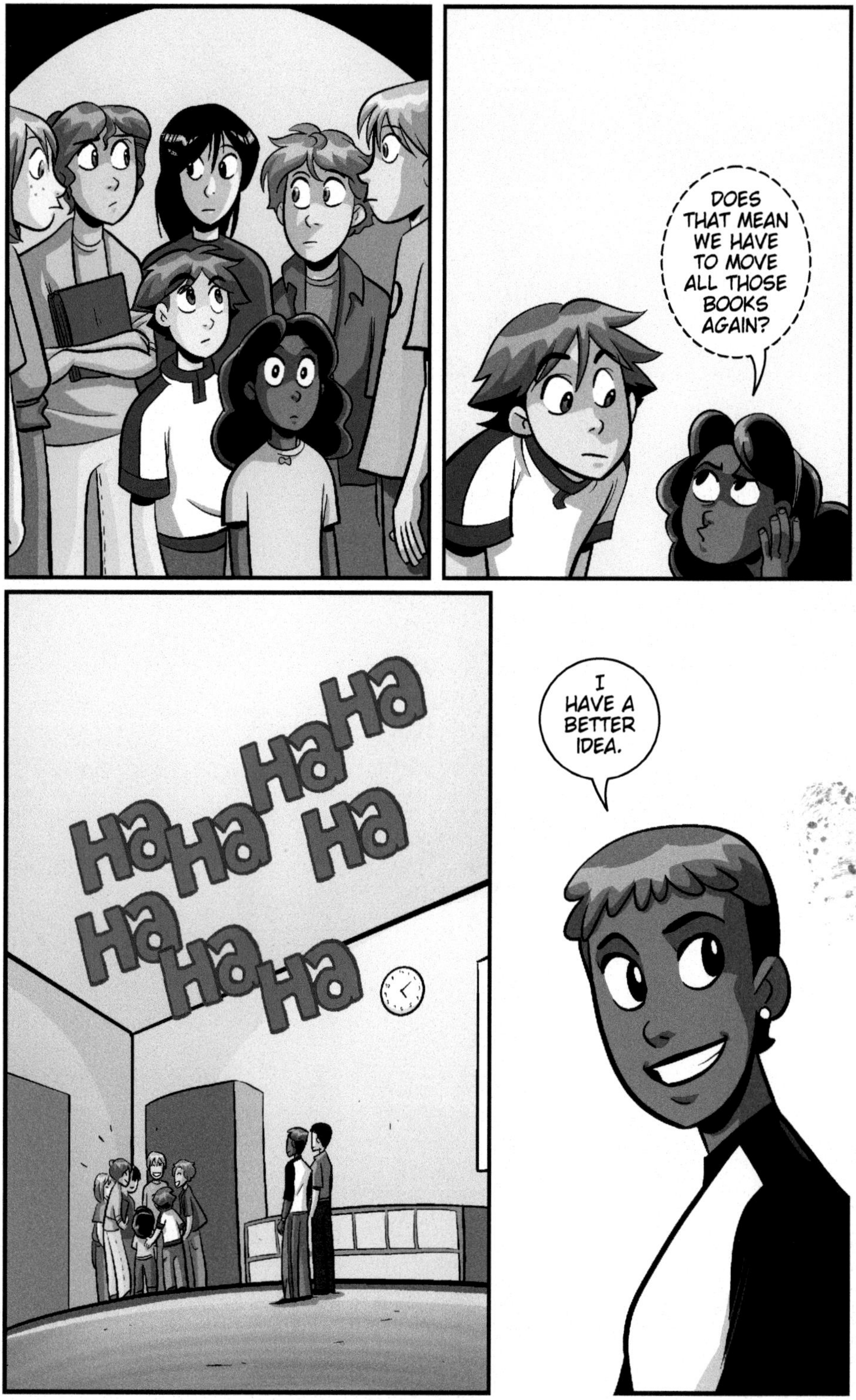
DOES THAT MEAN WE HAVE TO MOVE ALL THOSE BOOKS AGAIN?
HaHaHaHaHa Ha
HaHaHa
I HAVE A BETTER IDEA.

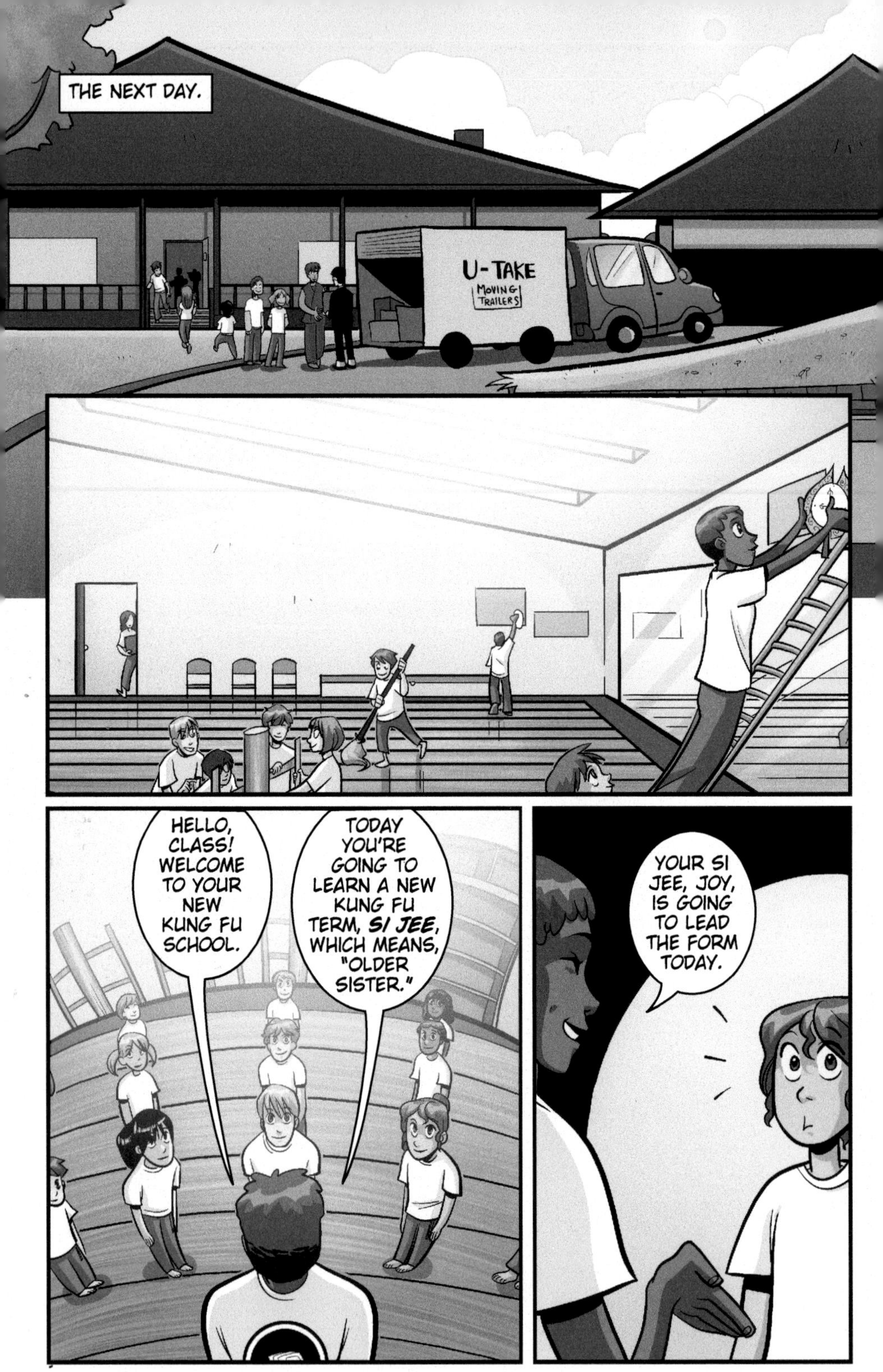

THE NEXT DAY.
U-TAKE
MOVING TRAILERS
HELLO, CLASS! WELCOME TO YOUR NEW KUNG FU SCHOOL.
TODAY YOU'RE GOING TO LEARN A NEW KUNG FU TERM, SI JEE, WHICH MEANS, "OLDER SISTER."
YOUR SI JEE, JOY, IS GOING TO LEAD THE FORM TODAY.

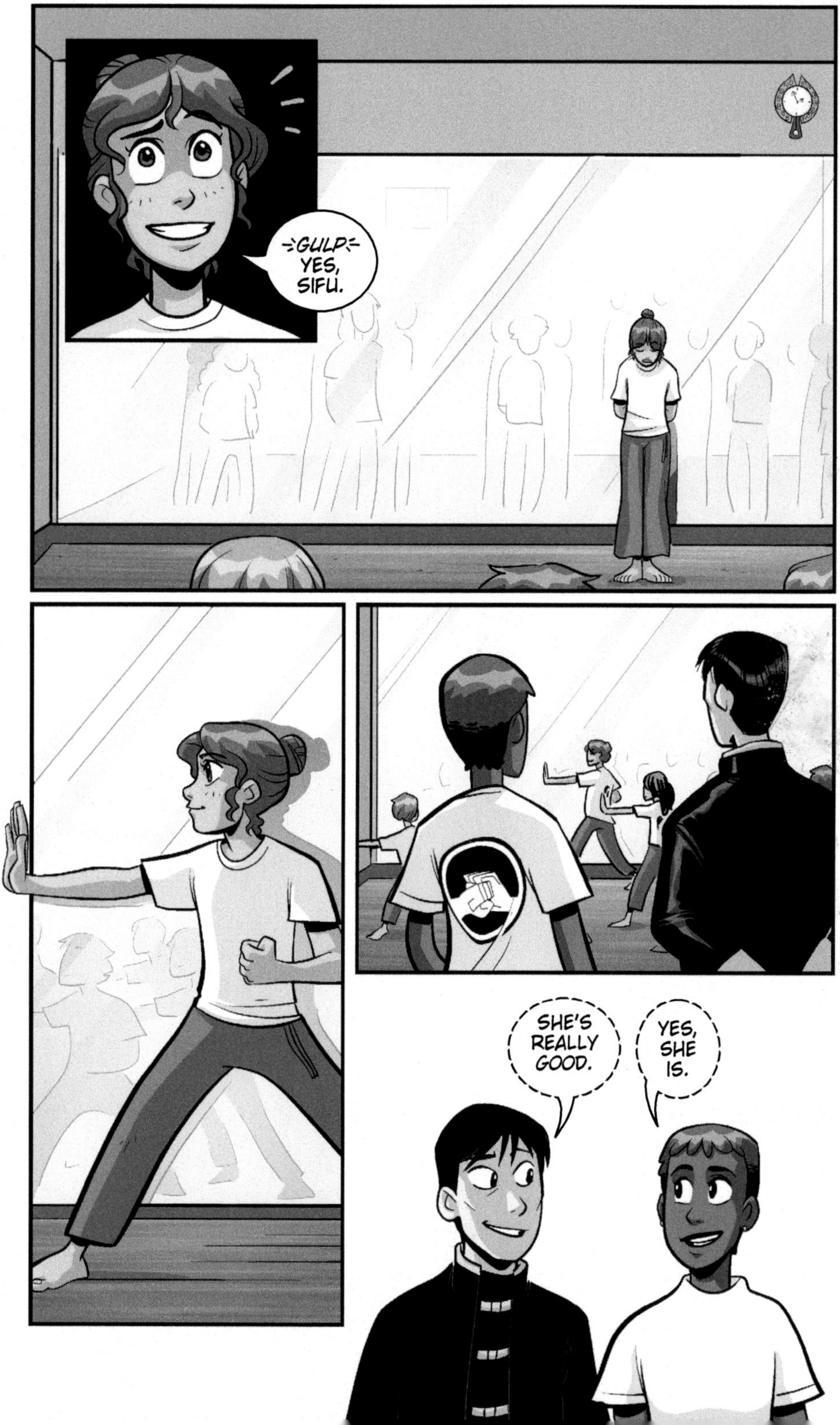

GULP
YES, SIFU.
SHE'S REALLY GOOD.
YES, SHE IS.

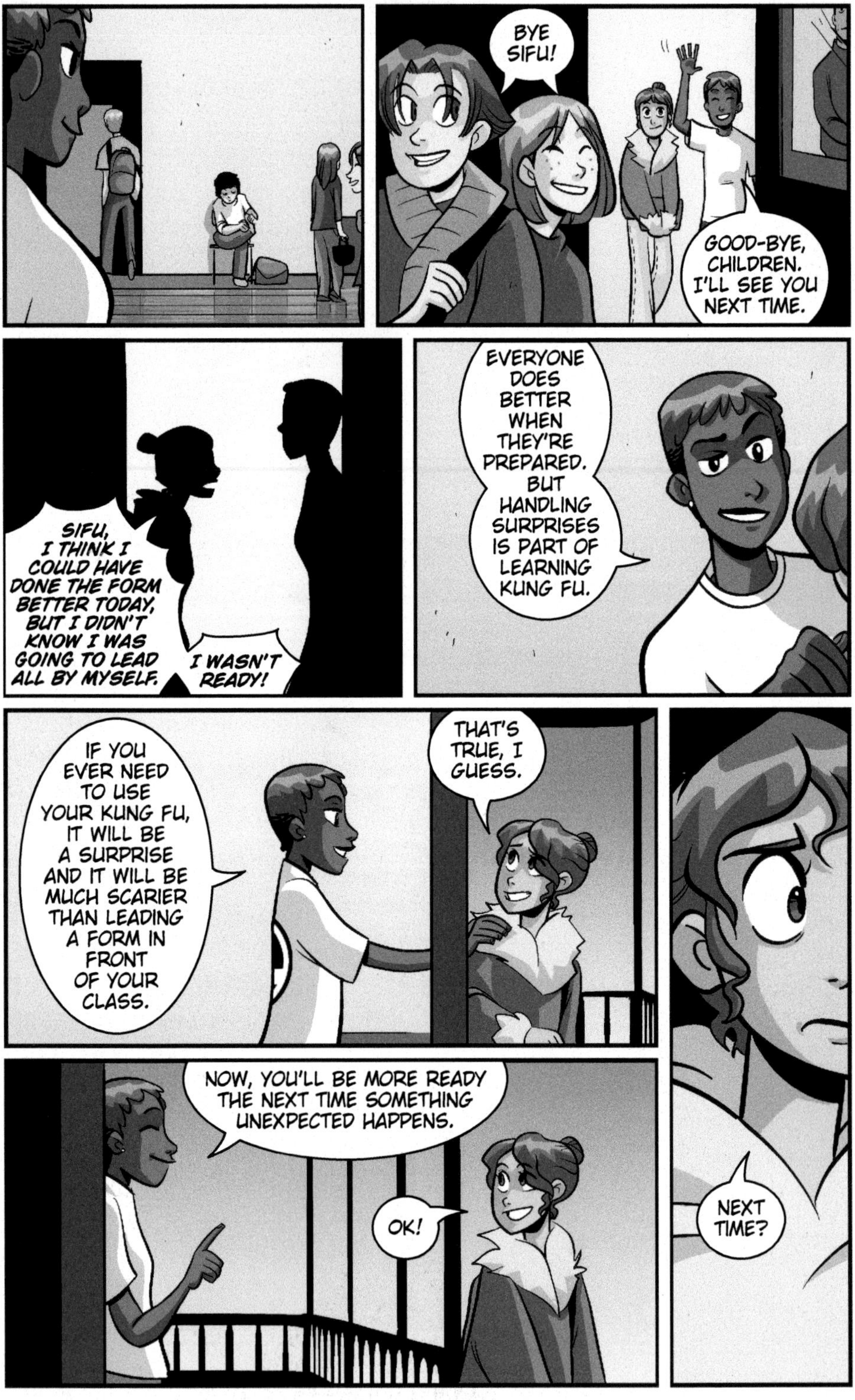
BYE SIFU!
GOOD-BYE, CHILDREN. I'LL SEE YOU NEXT TIME.
SIFU, I THINK I COULD HAVE DONE THE FORM BETTER TODAY, BUT I DIDN'T KNOW I WAS GOING TO LEAD ALL BY MYSELF.
I WASN'T READY!
EVERYONE DOES BETTER WHEN THEY'RE PREPARED. BUT HANDLING SURPRISES IS PART OF LEARNING KUNG FU.
IF YOU EVER NEED TO USE YOUR KUNG FU, IT WILL BE A SURPRISE AND IT WILL BE MUCH SCARIER THAN LEADING A FORM IN FRONT OF YOUR CLASS.
THAT'S TRUE, I GUESS.
NOW, YOU'LL BE MORE READY THE NEXT TIME SOMETHING UNEXPECTED HAPPENS.
OK!
NEXT TIME?

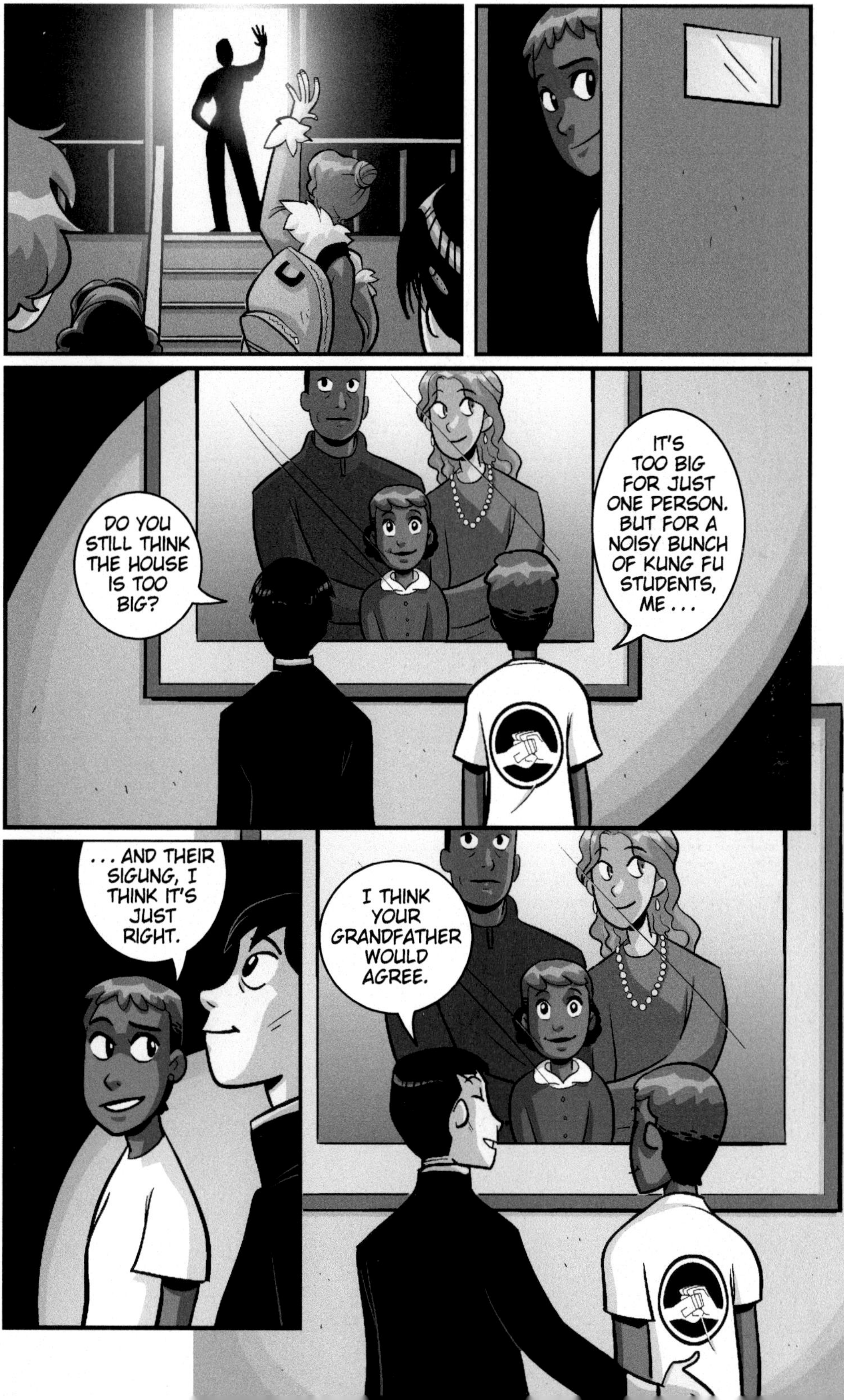
DO YOU STILL THINK THE HOUSE IS TOO BIG?
IT'S TOO BIG FOR JUST ONE PERSON. BUT FOR A NOISY BUNCH OF KUNG FU STUDENTS, ME . . .
. . . AND THEIR SIGUNG, I THINK IT'S JUST RIGHT.
I THINK YOUR GRANDFATHER WOULD AGREE.

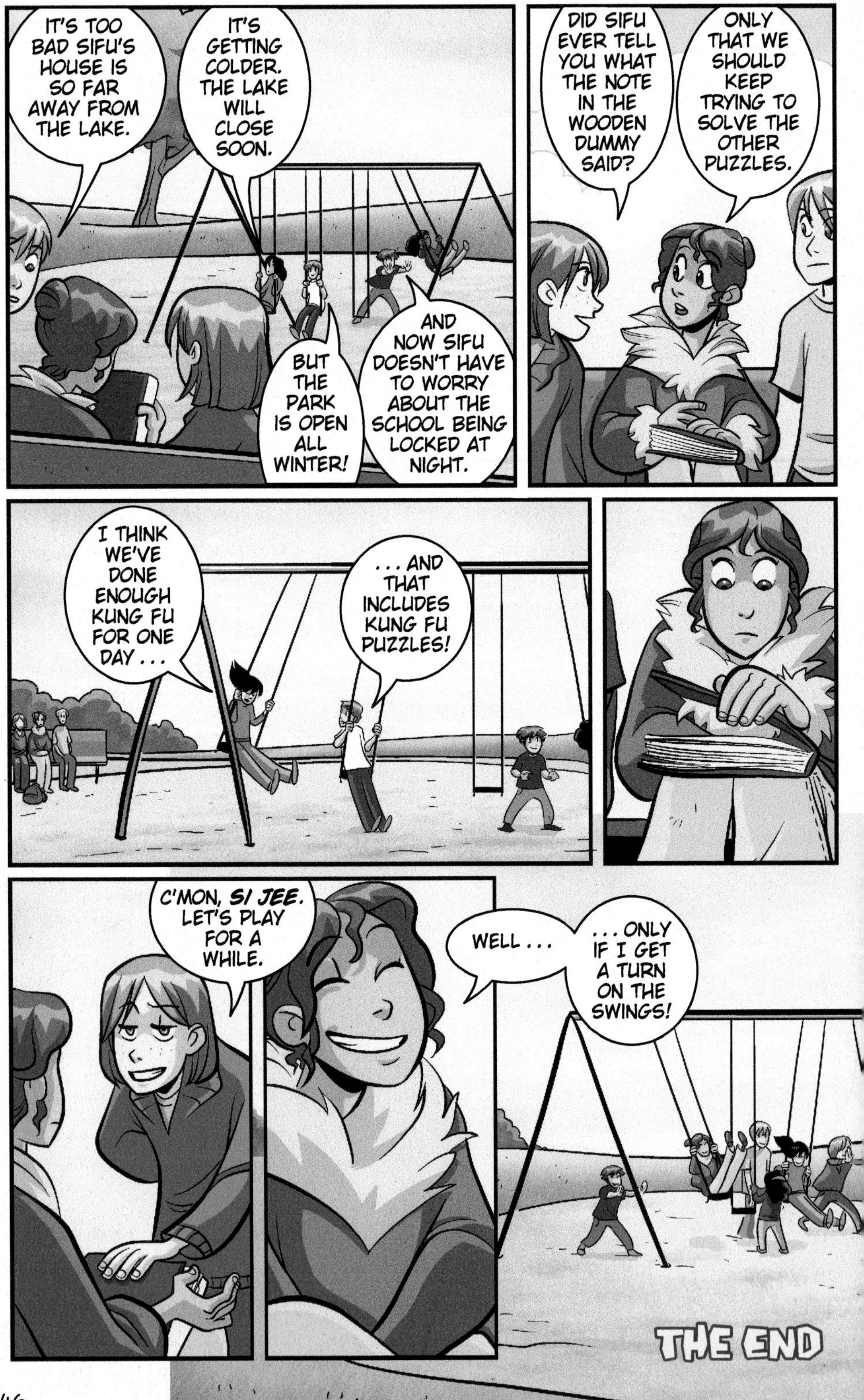
IT'S TOO BAD SIFU'S HOUSE IS SO FAR AWAY FROM THE LAKE.
IT'S GETTING COLDER. THE LAKE WILL CLOSE SOON.
BUT THE PARK IS OPEN ALL WINTER!
AND NOW SIFU DOESN'T HAVE TO WORRY ABOUT THE SCHOOL BEING LOCKED AT NIGHT.
DID SIFU EVER TELL YOU WHAT THE NOTE IN THE WOODEN DUMMY SAID?
ONLY THAT WE SHOULD KEEP TRYING TO SOLVE THE OTHER PUZZLES.
I THINK WE'VE DONE ENOUGH KUNG FU FOR ONE DAY . . .
. . . AND THAT INCLUDES KUNG FU PUZZLES!
C'MON, ***SI JEE***. LET'S PLAY FOR A WHILE.
WELL . . .
. . . ONLY IF I GET A TURN ON THE SWINGS!
THE END

The Author

Melinda Thielbar is a teacher who has written math courses for all ages, from kids to adults. In 2005 Melinda was awarded a VIGRE fellowship at North Carolina State University for PhD candidates "likely to make a strong contribution to education in mathematics." She lives in Raleigh, North Carolina, with her husband, author and video game programmer Richard Dansky, and their two cats.

The Artists

Tintin Pantoja was born in Manila in the Philippines. She received a degree in illustration and cartooning from the School of Visual Arts in New York City and was nominated for the Friends of Lulu "Best Newcomer" award. She was also a finalist in Tokyopop's Rising Stars of Manga 5. Her past books include a graphic novel version for kids of Shakespeare's play *Hamlet*.

Yuko Ota graduated from the Rochester Institute of Technology and lives in Maryland. She has worked as an animator and a lab assistant but is happiest drawing creatures and inventing worlds. She likes strong tea, the smell of new tires, and polydactyl cats (cats with extra toes!). She doesn't have any pets, but she has seven houseplants named Blue, Wolf, Charlene, Charlie, Roberto, Steven, and Doris.

Der-shing Helmer graduated with a degree in biology from UC Berkeley, where she played with snakes and lizards all summer long. She is working toward becoming a biology teacher. When she is not tutoring kids, she likes to create art, especially comics. Her best friends are her two pet geckos (Smeg and Jerry), her king snake (Clarice), and the chinchilla that lives next door.

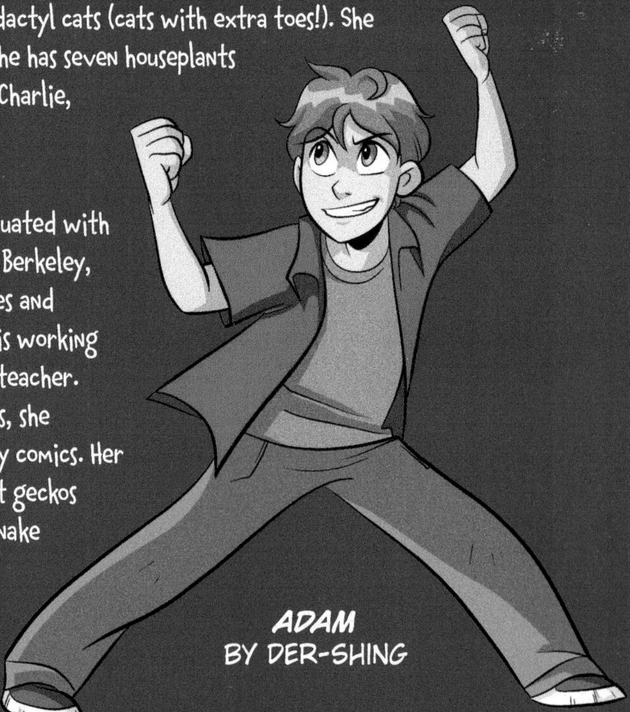

ADAM
BY DER-SHING

START READING FROM THE OTHER SIDE OF THE BOOK!

This page would be the first page of a manga from Japan. This is because written Japanese is read from the right side of the page to the left side of the page.

English is read from left to right, so this is the last page of this Manga Math Mystery. If you read the end of the book first, you'll spoil the mystery! Turn the book over so you can start on the first page. Then find the clues to the mystery with the kids from the kung fu school.

JOIN THE KIDS FROM THE KUNG FU SCHOOL IN SOLVING ALL THE MANGA MATH MYSTERIES!

ART BY TINTIN PANTOJA

MANGA MATH MYSTERIES